To Keeley

From Graham

(Author)

D1809093

ABOUT THE AUTHOR

Dr Graham Clingbine has BSc and MSc degrees from the University of London in the areas of Biological Science and Neurobiology respectively. His award of PhD followed a research programme on the memory mechanisms of the brain. Dr Clingbine spent a long career in education at schools and colleges before retiring from City & Islington College in North London where he held a post as Senior Lecturer and Course Manager of the Medical Access course.

Dr Clingbine has co-authored a number of paperback model answer books related to biology examination questions. He has a keen interest and extensive research knowledge in the subject area of unidentified flying objects (UFOs) and related phenomena including alien abductions and alleged secret governmental conspiracy theories which may be covering up cases of alien contact.

Dr Clingbine has a number of interests and hobbies but uppermost among these is fishing. He not only enjoys fishing the rivers, canals, lakes and seas of his home country (the UK) but has ventured further afield to countries across Europe and the USA.

RELEASE FROM STASIS

THE FUTURE IS NOW

DR GRAHAM CLINGBINE

Matador
9 Priory Business Park,
Wistow Road, Kibworth Beauchamp,
Leicestershire. LE8 0RX
Tel: 0116 279 2299
Email: books@troubador.co.uk
Web: www.troubador.co.uk/matador
Twitter: @matadorbooks

PB ISBN 978 1784625 283
HB ISBN 978 1784625 474

British Library Cataloguing in Publication Data.
A catalogue record for this book is available from the British Library.

Printed and bound by CPI Group (UK) Ltd, Croydon, CR0 4YY
Typeset in 11pt Aldine401 BT Roman by Troubador Publishing Ltd, Leicester, UK

Matador is an imprint of Troubador Publishing Ltd

The story is dedicated to people who have been important in my life story, some of whom have given me advice or feedback with respect to writing my books:

My wife Raby

My daughter Gemma Sara Clingbine
My daughter Lorraine Reed, grandchildren Jade,
Rebecca and Hayley and son-in-law Darren Reed

My parents Rose Bluma Clingbine (nee Goodman) and Joseph Samuel Clingbine (sadly no longer with us).

My brother David Clingbine and sister in law Pam Clingbine
Niece and nephew Sharon and Daniel and their families

I would also like to include a complimentary mention of the field workers, publications, television programmes and documentaries which have shed light over the years on unexplained paranormal phenomena and other enigmatic areas especially in the areas of UFO sightings, alien abductions, ancient astronauts, alleged governmental conspiracy theories and 'black ops'.

CONTENTS

INTRODUCTION AND BACKGROUND

'Release from Stasis: The Future is Now' is a sequel. It is a follow-on story from a previous publication called 'Disclosure: The Future is Now'. The latter is a fictional story which traces the life of Kevin Powell. The original story begins during Kevin's childhood when he is aged eight and living with his single mum, Sylvie. Kevin undergoes a number of strange experiences which his young mind cannot interpret and he assumes are a normal part of growing up. Kevin enters his teenage years and supports his mum when she falls ill and requires surgery to remove a mysterious implanted object. In his adulthood, he courts and marries Jane. They have a beautiful daughter called Amy. Kevin has a number of realistic nightmare-like visions in which he sees his wife and mum in a bizarre unfamiliar environment. Revelations are shown to him from a distant future depopulated planet Earth. Kevin has to face a difficult dilemma. He needs to decide whether to comply with his father John's plan to save mankind and repopulate a future barren planet Earth or resist his wishes and save his daughter Amy from becoming part of his father's programme.

'Release from Stasis: The Future is Now' can be enjoyed equally well after reading 'Disclosure: The Future is Now', or by itself. It stands alone in its own right as an interesting story without any necessity for reading its predecessor. The reader will become fully immersed in the plot as events unfold and not want to put the book down until reaching the shocking culmination of the 'Release from Stasis'.

LEGACY

Misinformation and alleged government cover ups need to be ended in the area of UFO sightings, alien contacts and related phenomena. The people of the world and citizens of the international community of nations deserve to know the truth of both 'what is out there' and what is really happening in the 'here and now'. Disclosure and transparency are long overdue. The history of UFO sightings and reported crash-retrievals, alien abductions and so on has been shrouded by a cloak of governmental misinformation and strange enigmatic 'black ops' for too long. The subject area is often laughed at and not taken seriously by many members of the public...the 'little green man' syndrome of the media. Even if UFO sightings are due to mass hysteria, Venus, swamp gas or flocks of birds, thousands of witnesses are recording images on camcorders and suchlike. Is there a worldwide psychological delusion occurring? The fictional stories of events in the future featured in my previous book Disclosure and here in Release From Stasis about how the Earth may become altered could become a reality. Novel technology such as nerve implants, time portals, star gates, reversible wormhole travel, faster than light-speed craft and teleportation may become realities. This is not just fantasy but genuine speculation of future events born from the growing knowledge, understanding and possibilities derived from the Theory of Relativity, warping spacetime, string theory, multidimensions, multiuniverses, cybernetics, nanotechnology, robotics, the existence of dark matter and dark energy, matter-antimatter, subatomic particles, space medicine and space exploration.

My wishes for revelation of the truth in the areas mentioned above can be summed up by the commonly used instruction by the science fiction character Captain Jean Luc Picard of the Star Trek series... "Make it so." Read on...and enjoy!

FOREWORD

Consider humankind existing in the distant future. Perhaps they are the extraterrestrials speculated to exist following anomalous sightings on planet Earth of today. Maybe it is ourselves in a different anatomical guise who are the 'visitors' sometimes seen as occupants of strange aerial UFOs and embarking from or returning to craft on the ground. The strange looking aliens purported to abduct humans may be people from our own future or another dimension involved in some unknown task, study or experiment. It is more than possible that 'the future is now'.

The technological advances and inventions of the last couple of hundred years would seem like fantasy to older generations. Likewise, the people of our present generation would be awestruck by technology of entities hundreds or perhaps thousands of years in advance of our own. Current day reactions to phenomena like UFO sightings often involve ridicule or debunking by many individuals. Those that do accept UFO sightings as real but inexplicable events often show not only amazement but sometimes also fear. Even educated intelligent individuals in our modern society have no real understanding of the way observed exotic craft make amazing turns at high velocity, come to a standstill in mid-air or change shape and texture. Some of these incredible observations include sightings of giant motherships spewing forth smaller scout ships. Possibly related to such observations, there are widespread reports of alien abductions and these also provoke a mixture of ridicule, fear and speculation. The apparent passage of abducted persons through solid objects into strange craft and the subsequent use of exotic medical probes to examine abductees is indeed mind boggling.

Perhaps we should not be quite so surprised and shocked at these amazing but strange events. After all, present day scientists are already discussing the concept of warping spacetime in order to travel vast distances via wormholes. There is real scientific speculation about time warps, star gates and exotic engine drive systems which might use matter-antimatter or antigravity propulsion. The knowledge of subatomic particles has led to 'string theory' which increases the likelihood of the existence of multidimensions and a multiverse in which more than one universe co-exist. The existence of more than one reality is now not as improbable as once believed. It is not in the realms of impossibility that one day we might be able to slip into the past or future and return, perhaps to change the course of history. As mentioned, some believe that the beings often described during abductions are in fact not alien at all but humankind from the future or other dimensions. New scientific concepts and imaginative speculation related to such ideas are used in the context of the story in this book.

Ancient civilizations seem to have jumped quickly from primitive cave-dwelling to complex social societies with remarkable building and engineering works. The pyramids and temples of the Sumerians, ancient Egyptians and Mayans represent amazing archaeological achievements. How could such complex building work have been carried out without modern technological knowledge and equipment? Where did they get advanced knowledge of mathematics and astronomy from? Why are there so many ancient paintings with artwork which resemble modern implements like planes and helicopters? Why are there images of people looking like men in spacesuits and sketches resembling UFOs? How come so many ancient scrolls and manuscripts have stories of Gods' descending from the skies or stars? It is possible that ancient astronauts have visited the Earth for thousands of years or people from our future have travelled back in time to oversee human development. Many speculate that genetic engineering many generations ago contributed to mankind's development.

The Cosmos contains vast numbers of stars and more and more planets orbiting them are being discovered on a regular basis. Many of these planets may have suitable conditions to sustain life. How likely is it that humankind exists alone as the only form of intelligent life? Frank Drake in 1961 produced an argument defined by what has become known as the Drake Equation. This gives an estimate of the number of active, communicative extraterrestrial civilizations in the Milky Way galaxy and the estimate is substantial. Life on other planets with advanced technology is not only likely but may be commonplace.

Stars are suns powered by nuclear fusion in which hydrogen is converted into helium. Such stars may remain hot, bright and stable for five billion years or more. Our sun is often grouped as a yellow dwarf. Young stars are classified as dwarfs, yellow dwarfs and red dwarfs. As stars begin to die they become supergiants, red giants and blue giants. Some may explode and develop into a supernova or they may eventually form white dwarfs. Faint and virtually dead stars include white dwarfs, brown dwarfs, neutron stars and pulsars.

Some suns also exist as binary stars. In a double star system, two stars may either just appear close to each other in the sky or actually revolve around one another. A true binary star is when two stars revolve around a common centre of mass known as a barycentre, an example being the Pole Star of Earth's Northern Hemisphere. There are other categories of binary stars including eclipsing binaries, X-ray binaries, cepheid binaries and mira variables.

Readers interested to know more about the categories of stars, how they are born and die or any other astronomical phenomena such as black holes, event horizons, dark matter, dark energy and antimatter should seek out astronomical reference sources. Some of these terms are used in this book.

In the story of this book, the Earth's future sun has aged and lost its stability, appearing large and red in a black, mainly starless sky. The sun is bombarding the Earth with deadly solar particles.

CHAPTER 1

The Future is Now: A Scene Without a View

John Powell inhaled deeply. It was not easy. In fact, breathing was becoming a conscious effort. How had it come to this? The Great Plan needed to succeed. In fact, it needed to succeed very quickly or it would be too late. So many brilliant minds had planned a route to survival. Now he stood alone. John would need to amend his own ideas on what to do. Survival on the Earth depended on his actions. He was struggling. If he died it would be the end for mankind. This was not an option. It could not be allowed to happen. He had to continue to live and fulfil his mission.

The responsibility weighed heavily on John's shoulders. He was unsure why he felt such a heavy burden. After all, there was no-one left to be accountable to. Perhaps he was driven by an inborn moral compass. Maybe he had to honour the efforts of his former colleagues. They had been great scientists and engineers. Their knowledge was bountiful. Now they were all dead.

John surveyed the scene. This was a futuristic Earth. This was an Earth unrecognisable to those that lived in the distant past. Lush green landscapes were long since gone forever. There were no vast oceans or flowing rivers, no mountain ranges or forests. Perhaps in its own way this place was beautiful. Even if this was true, it seemed as if the Earth had become a final giant graveyard for mankind and abetted by the sun wanted to rid itself of the hominid parasite that walked upon it. It seemed that the final demise of humankind in world history was nigh.

John stood on flat ground. Beneath his feet was a blue-green grassy surface. This was not natural grass. The original range of grass species had perished long ago along with the other forms of terrestrial life. In an effort to keep some kind of link to the old world, scientists had genetically engineered this layer which coated the barren ground below it. It was a living layer of artificially synthesised plant material. It had been placed over the landscape much in the same way as a carpet covers a living room floor. Even synthetic grass felt better to walk on than a rocky stratum. It pleased the eye. The alternative was much worse. There were no trees, shrubs or flowers. This Earth could not sustain them. At least this surface coating gave some kind of characterization to the flat landscape. There were no mountains, no hills or valleys, just a flat blue-green sheet stretching out to the horizon. One redeeming feature was that it could nourish itself using novel metabolic pathways that carried out a version of photosynthesis installed into it by gene splicing the DNA from a range of now extinct plants.

John cast his eyes upwards. Only one feature dominated overhead. It was a large blood red orb. It stood overhead in a black sky. The stars had long ago continued flying apart from each other rather like a single point on the skin of a balloon moving outwards when it stretches on inflation. Virtually nothing twinkled overhead except for an occasional straggler, a star lagging behind its colleagues as they flew away from each other in an expanding Universe. The red sun was perhaps three times the diameter of the old ancestral version of the solar body. That old version of the sun had a powerful nuclear reactor in its core. The ancient 'solar lady' was bright and life sustaining. Her solar energy provided light and heat to living Gaia. The old Earth eventually had evolved with the ageing of the sun into its final futuristic form. John was able to look directly at the red expanded solar orb above him without the need for eye protection. The dull light rays did not impinge harmfully on his retina. They did not have the strength to do so.

This was a quiet place. There was no breeze to ruffle ones clothes. No gusts of wind blew through fields of wheat to make them sway in waves across expansive open fields. This air was still. It had the feel of stagnancy. No birds or other animal life filled the skies or landscape. There was a deafening silence.

John surveyed the scene which was not completely devoid of objects. To his left, perhaps a mile away, lay the only surviving building. It had been constructed by his deceased colleagues as a special place. It was vital for the success of the Great Plan. It was a massive spherical oasis in a desert of green-blue. It had a glasslike translucent outer wall which partially concealed what lay inside. John would soon make his way back to the building to continue his lone task.

Another object was visible far distant to John's right side. The object was a pyramid which stood a little higher than a human. Its facing wall had a triangular shape. Inbuilt into this structure was a 'doorway' which was not readily visible to the naked eye. This object was not a building. It was a technological marvel of the future. In the old days this exotic machine would have been called a time portal. It was tried and tested. In fact, John had used the device very frequently.

The device had the fantastic ability to warp spacetime. It would allow temporal interdimensional jumps to those who passed across its interface. John took some time to reflect on the use he had made of it. He had used it to visit the old Earth at various times in its history. The agenda for the Great Plan had been put into action. He had carefully selected genetically appropriate human specimens and brought them into his future time. Whether this had an ethical issue around it or not had not concerned John until his son Kevin produced a moral argument against such activities. These people had not volunteered to leave their past lives, they were forcibly taken. John had managed to alter their memories by means of an implant embedded into their nervous system. This implant produced 'screen memories' which masked and suppressed their original ones. It also gave him a means of mind control and communication. Since the abductees had no memories of their previous lives they would not be psychologically damaged. What they did not remember would not worry them. John had obtained a good collection of not only men and women but also children. He needed good breeding stock both now and in the future. He would give further consideration to his son Kevin's moral arguments at a future time. There was no time to waste implementing the Great Plan.

John had taken a historical female from the old Earth as his mate. Sylvie was now located deep within the spherical building. However, their son Kevin was residing on the old Earth in a previous historical time. Kevin had been brought into the future Earth by his father and informed of its dire situation. John had given Kevin great scientific knowledge utilising an implant he had inserted into his son's neck. Vast quantities of information and data had been downloaded into Kevin's mind to enable him to carry out a role helping John to deliver the Great Plan for future Earth's survival.

Kevin had a daughter called Amy. John had great plans for Amy. His granddaughter had been genetically engineered by him to play a pivotal role in repopulating the future Earth. Her genetically manipulated reproductive cells would go a long way in a breeding programme towards the production of offspring with new characteristics which would aid survival in the changed Earthly conditions. John had not expected Kevin to argue a moral case for leaving Amy on the old Earth to live out her natural life there where she was popular and loved. Kevin had somehow resisted his implant's mind control and fought against his father's desire to transfer Amy when mature into the future. Kevin's love for his daughter Amy was most impressive.

John eventually decided to concede to his son's moral arguments, at least as far as Amy was concerned. He allowed his granddaughter to remain in the past with Kevin and fulfil her lifespan there. This presented a major problem for the Great Plan. John would have to develop a new strategy to save the world from human extinction but his newly found compassion for others was an eye opener to him. John was proud of his son. Kevin had made him aware that as a person existing as a human in the future, he had undergone a decline in his emotions and feelings of care for others. These attributes in Kevin's view were an intrinsic part of being human.

Due to the legacy of an encounter in which John had translocated Kevin, his wife Sylvie and Kevin's wife Jane into his own time on the future Earth, he now physically had the body of his wife and daughter-in-law in his possession. He had managed to keep them alive and both Sylvie and Jane resided in the spherical building while Kevin had been returned to the past. John had planned that Kevin would nurture his daughter until she was at a suitably mature physical stage ready for him to utilise his granddaughter's genes in the laudable Great Plan to save mankind. John's change of heart in leaving granddaughter Amy to live out her life with her dad Kevin on the old Earth would in due course lead John to alternative drastic experimentation.

As the sun changed, the Earth changed with it. The terrestrial environment gradually altered in brightness, temperature, humidity and so on. Even particles from space, cosmic rays and ultraviolet light had gradually penetrated the atmosphere and reached the surface. The protective ozone layer was much depleted. Human genes had mutated and the process of survival of the fittest in the changed environment had occurred. The best adapted individuals survived and those least well adapted gradually died off. Genetic death followed. The traits of those that had died were removed from the gene pool of the population. When natural selection began to negatively affect human survival, scientists set about manipulating the human genome. Genetic engineering techniques manipulated the genes such that artificial selection of favoured individuals encouraged their survival in an increasingly hostile Earthly environment. John was one such artificially genetically manipulated survivor. In fact, he was now the last survivor. That is why he alone had to implement the Great Plan.

John's physical anatomy was not the same as those who had lived on the old Earth. The old human physical form had followed the usual laws of natural selection and changed with the passage of time. John's body was quite well adapted to the surroundings. He had a somewhat bulbous bald head attached to a delicate torso. He had long and slender limbs. He did not have well defined or heavy musculature. The force of gravity was low and did not require a well developed musculoskeletal system. His eyes were very large, slanted, dark and without eyelids. The level of illumination was low and bright light would in fact have dazzled him and made vision uncomfortable. There were no extraneous dust or other particles in the air and so protective eyelid blink reflexes were not needed. Outer ear structures such as pinnae (ear flaps and lobes) were absent but a small vestigial orifice was present on each side of the head. John's reduced nose had tiny openings for nostrils which led to a specialised respiratory system capable of utilising the lowered levels of oxygen in the air. John's brain was expanded with an increased surface area in the cerebral cortex. The extensive folded surface reflected his great intelligence and knowledge. He, along with his deceased peers, had developed a telepathic ability and it was no longer necessary to vocalise sounds in order to communicate.

Green plants which once released oxygen gas into the atmosphere were now gone. The artificially created blue-green grass did release some oxygen as a by-product of metabolism but also some sulphur-containing gases which left an odour of 'gone off' eggs. John's mouth was little more than a slit and his gut system was minimal. Nutrients could be absorbed directly through his surface grey-blue skin layers by diffusion following immersion in or exposure to a fluid nutritive medium. Male genitalia were present but rather resembled the clasper structures of fish in the shark family.

Despite the best efforts of scientists, the Earth's environment was still changing, making adaptation nearly impossible despite the best efforts of the genetic engineers. The great minds and visionaries that were once John's colleagues were now gone. John was beginning to find breathing somewhat more difficult outside the spherical building and his own future survival was in doubt.

The environment inside the building was artificially controlled. Within the building a low level of illumination was maintained. The oxygen levels were higher than outside and the temperature was kept at a constant seventy degrees Celsius. An artificial system also gave a degree of humidity to the air and sophisticated equipment recycled water supplies. Survival of old style *Homo sapiens* was possible inside the building for the likes of John's wife Sylvie and daughter-in-law Jane. The conditions were within both their and John's homeostatic range of tolerance but life outside of the building was becoming increasingly difficult for John and strictly time limited for old style humans. John considered himself to be a variant of old style humankind and thought of himself as *Homo sapiens futuralis*.

It had become clear to John that the world outside the spherical building would not support human life as it existed for much longer. A repopulation programme would need to make use of engineered hybrids. These could be produced by manipulating the DNA of his abducted residential old style humans and utilising their extracted sperms and ova in breeding programmes. Eventually, he hoped the environmentally well adapted new human hybrids could be released to colonise the changing Earth. However, the ongoing changes in the nature of the atmosphere were making John's Great Plan increasingly difficult, if not impossible, to successfully complete. Another way might have to be found.

John made his way towards the spherical building. Walking was very easy. It was more like an off ground floating movement and his feet only required occasional light contact with the surface to propel him forwards. The low gravity enabled almost effortless locomotion. As John approached the outer wall of the building, a section of the surface changed in texture due to atomic reconfiguration, enabling him to pass through it into the building. The building itself was huge and had a great domed roof. The roof had an intrinsic glow giving a dull illumination to everything that lay below it.

The building contained a maze-like network of corridors. Many of these had small side rooms used for various functions and procedures. There were also ramps leading upwards to higher levels. Some of the corridors opened out into large rooms resembling hospital surgical theatres with exotic operating tables which could float, move and tilt extensively. All manner of probes and devices for medical investigation, experimentation or treatment were suspended overhead or near the tables.

After entering the building, John chose a route along a passageway to the right. He moved down a narrow tube-like corridor with a low ceiling. The corridor came to an end and John continued onwards into an expansive room, rectangular in shape. This room was somewhat better illuminated than the corridor which fed into it and light appeared to emanate directly from the surrounding walls. The room contained a series of upright rectangular vats positioned along the walls. The vats were closed off along the sides and base. A device hovered over the open upper surface which resembled a hoist-like machine. This could grab a human body and lower it down into or raise it out of the vat. Each vat contained enough space to place an adult human body with just enough room for it to stand upright.

Most of the vats were filled with human bodies, one per vat. They were not corpses but vibrant moving torsos that moved their arms and legs wildly and frequently. The bodies were completely naked and totally enveloped by viscous, syrupy semi-liquid. Oxygenating bubbles rose upwards from the base of the vat to its roof before dissipating. Many of the vat-enclosed people jammed themselves against the transparent front casing of their vat, twisting or contorting their naked bodies against it. Some even made sexual thrusting movements while others turned 360 degrees, briefly exposing their bare buttocks as they rotated. All the people had their eyes wide open but none of them showed any sign of cognition and their eyes focussed on imaginary distant objects.

The vats contained humans representing all the ethnic and racial groups on the old Earth. The men and women were sexually mature and healthy appearing specimens. The vats lined up along the left hand wall of the room contained males. Their naked bodies were bathed by an emerald green version of the viscous syrup. A short time earlier, John had lowered a device into the vats which clamped tightly over the genitals of the men and violated them. The machine extracted semen samples and then stored them in overhead containers above each vat until required for genetic experimentation.

The right hand wall was lined by further vats and these were the ones containing the bodies of naked women. Two of these containers were the focus of John's attention as he had come especially to check on them. One of these contained the living body of his wife Sylvie and the adjacent one held Jane, his son Kevin's beautiful blonde wife. Neither of the women showed any sign of recognition or independent action. Like the men in the vats opposite them, they thrashed their arms and legs around in the syrupy liquid, gyrated their hips and from time to time rotated mindlessly in circles. The two women appeared to be in good physical condition. They both had at one time been given neural implants by which John controlled them and monitored their thoughts. The implants had now been surgically removed but their residual influence on the nervous system was still present and extraneous telepathic instruction would still generate limited neurogenic control as and when John decided it was required. The vats that contained all the women were similar to those of the men except that the embalming soupy fluid had a pink colouration due to a slight variation in constituency.

The men and women in this rectangular room were the prime ones used most recently in John's genetic experimentation programme as part of the Great Plan. In one group of experiments, some of the males and females of contrasting racial stock were selected and paired off in a eugenic selective breeding programme. The hoist-like machines would lower themselves into the vats and carefully grip and remove required human bodies and place them in front of their containers. Under mind control of the implants surgically placed in their neural tissue, the people would be instructed to walk a short distance along the incoming corridor and turn into a small cul-de-sac where the female would be instructed to lie down on a legless supporting table-like surface. The couple were then instructed to partake in sexual intercourse before being returned to their vats. In due course the woman would show signs of pregnancy and would then be monitored until full term. After giving birth, the baby would be taken away and assessed for adaptability and survival value in the future Earth's environment. The baby itself would then be placed in a storage vat and monitored as it developed through childhood towards maturity.

Another part of the genetic study programme involved the temporary removal of a selected female from the vat. She would be directed to one of the large surgical theatre like rooms. Once there, a surgical probe would be passed through her naval region to withdraw her eggs. When the procedure was over, the woman would be returned to her storage vat. The eggs and selected sperm from a particular male would then undergo an *in vitro* fertilization procedure. Sometimes genetic intervention would take place involving gene splicing and gene recombination. The genetically manipulated zygote would be placed into a surrogate mother to develop inside her body and again at the end of the pregnancy following birth, the infant could be studied, monitored and stored.

The wall facing the incoming corridor and separating the males and females were lined with vats containing developing children immersed in an orange supportive medium. They ranged from the newborn to pre-pubic boys and girls. Some of these children were hybrids. Frozen sperm samples from his deceased futuristic male colleagues were used to impregnate stored human females from the old Earth. The children showed characteristics in-between *Homo sapiens* and *Homo sapiens futuralis*. For example, some had old style human facial features with dark black slanted, almond shaped eyes while others had normal eyes on a bulbous bald head and elongated slender body.

John had no ethical qualms about such experiments. His only motivation was to repopulate the ailing future Earth. However, his view had become clouded as mentioned earlier, following a conversational moral disagreement with his son

Kevin about such experimentation. As a result of this, John had modified his plans for his wife Sylvie and Jane, his daughter-in-law. His wife Sylvie had been a supportive partner during their time together on the old Earth. She had borne him a fine son. He hoped to be able to release her from the stasis state which sustained her in her vat so that she could rejoin him among the new humankind population he would set free into the new Earthly environment. This might be possible following appropriate physical changes he would make to her anatomy and physiology to aid her survival.

John had planned to bring Amy, the daughter of his son Kevin and his wife Jane, into his future as a key part of the survival programme. He had already genetically modified his granddaughter Amy. However, he had allowed her to return to the past to live out her childhood and young adulthood under the care of Kevin. John had been intent on bringing a sexually developed and matured Amy into the future to participate in the release stage of the Great Plan. However, his newly acquired compassion caused him to allow Amy to remain with her dad Kevin in the past and get on with her life without interference.

What was he to do with Kevin's wife Jane? Perhaps he would send her back through the time portal into the past to rejoin her husband and meet her now grown up daughter, Amy. He had not decided her fate yet.

John was no stranger himself to life within a stasis storage vat. His colleagues and compatriots had done their utmost to make the physical and anatomical modifications to survive the changing Earthly environment. However, further swift changes in atmospheric composition took a rapid unexpected toll of lives and the already low human population took a further rapid and irreversible decline in numbers. John was fortunately relatively resistant and resilient to the environmental changes. His colleagues decided to place him in his own storage vat where he would be kept in stasis. After a number of years he would be automatically released from storage. It was hoped that the most recent changes to the atmospheric composition would be temporary or reversible. By the time John was released from stasis, he might be able to re-undertake the Great Plan. He had all the skills and knowledge to complete a repopulation programme.

On his release from stasis, John had embarked on the experimentation programme of the Great Plan for survival. He had achieved a measure of success but now once again the Earth's environment was changing and breathing was becoming uncomfortable. John was the lone survivor in this future Earth. His colleagues had perished several years before his release from the stasis vat. The continuing fluctuations in environmental conditions were already beginning to affect John adversely. This would throw a spanner in the works of the Great Plan.

CHAPTER 2

The Great Release

John peered across the large spherical building. He was located high up on a viewing platform. The results of his hard work were laid out before him. He observed the numerous storage vats filled with living bodies spread out at different levels. In fact, there were thousands of them. John had been following the Great Plan for some time and had been very industrious in his efforts. Not only had he been deeply involved in his genetic manipulation studies but he had surpassed himself in his expectations of collecting suitable human specimens from the old Earth.

John had made full use of futuristic technology to make jumps through the time portal into the past. He had visited various historical ages in times gone past and also a range of geographical locations. This was done because of his requirement to collect human specimens of varied genetic diversity. His powers of telepathic mind control had enabled him to induce people to pass through the interface of the time portal into his future world. Once his specimens had been gathered, he undertook physiological and biochemical assessments of them. The process was automated and was carried out in the large rooms resembling medical theatres equipped with tables which held the abductees in place while diagnostic probes were inserted into their bodies. John was not only interested in the general health of his human subjects but also their genetic viability and genotype. Their genetic make up was very important. Suitable individuals would have their gametes extracted and these ova and sperm stored until required for breeding experimentation.

Once the analysis of an abducted individual was complete, John had to make a decision. If the person was unsuitable for his requirements, he would return them to their old life at their appropriate historical time and location. He would then relax his mind control. The person would temporarily feel confused or disorientated before resuming their everyday existence. They would invariably experience a sense of missing time. An hour or two had been taken from them and they had no idea where they had been or what they had been doing. Sometimes a screen memory was placed in an abductee's mind to give the false impression that he or she had been engaged in some activity or journey.

Many abductees who were returned to their own time suffered recurring unexplained nightmares and some of them subsequently underwent regression hypnosis sessions in an attempt to break through the screen memories and understand the cause of their bad dreams. The conducting hypnotist, usually a psychiatrist or psychologist (though sometimes a UFO researcher), would make sound and/ or videotaped recordings of the session. Usually the people investigating the abduction stories put them down to illusions, hallucinations, mental disorders, drug use, hysteria, disturbing dreams, paranoia and sleep paralysis. Sometimes the alleged abductee was considered to be a hoaxer or attention seeker. Any marks or wounds on the body claimed to have resulted from the claimed abduction experience were explained away one way or another. Many abduction victims recalled under hypnosis terrifying medical experimentation in a strange place by an alien creature but very few investigators accepted abduction claims and accounts at face value. The fact that abductees from different countries around the world were relating similar stories was ignored. Abduction accounts of people from first world advanced countries were put down to cultural influences of the time such as science fiction movies, television programmes and magazine stories. Most abductees preferred to stay silent to avoid the risk of being mocked or losing their employment.

Some of the abductees were deemed suitable for John's ongoing studies. Such individuals were not returned to their past life. They became 'missing persons'. When John felt he could make use of such a forcibly invited guest, he would use the facility's equipment to insert an implant into the nervous system. This was often done either in the neck region or directly into the fissures of the cerebral cortex. Each implant was a tiny pyramid shaped object made of rare metal alloys. The object was an advanced form of nanotechnology and barely discernible by old style scans and X-rays. Once the implant was inserted, John gained long term full control of the person. He could bend their will, control their movements and feed false memories into the individual. Also, he was able to 'download' information into the brain to re-educate the individual, amend their personality and monitor their DNA. John had collected a mass of human bodies taken from various points in time going all the way back to eras of pre-recorded human history and far beyond.

There were men, women and children of all racial groups in John's human collection. The key factor which determined whether specimens were retained in John's collection or not was their genetic composition. They had to have the potential to provide genes which might generate offspring with a new bodily phenotype and changed metabolism. It might be possible for some individuals with a changed bodily form and novel biological chemistry to be released into the future

Earth and survive in the changing environment. The adults John collected and retained made good breeding stock. He mainly collected sexually mature adults. These were fertile individuals from whom he could extract viable eggs and sperms or who could be made to mate and produce offspring for his studies. The children he collected would develop into future replacement sexually mature adults for further breeding studies.

John had a special interest in hybrid children. These children were formed by the fusion either of an old style female human egg with a sperm from a futuristic male or by using sperm from an old style Earth male and extracted egg donated by a female from the future time zone. Fertilization was carried out either by an *in vitro* dish technique or by inserting sperm samples into the uterus via the vagina and cervix. The sperms would start lashing their tails and swim naturally through the uterus into the oviduct in search of an ovum to fertilize. The human females served as incubation vessels or surrogate mothers to house and nurture developing embryos. Their children were delivered and then removed and taken away for investigation. Newly born babies were stored in vats and their development monitored. Surely individuals would be produced sooner or later that would thrive in the conditions on the future Earth and be able to repopulate it? That was John's hope.

John continued to survey the scene from his lofty perch high up in the dome of the spherical building. Away to his left and below him was vat after vat of naked men. They had all been removed from the old Earth and deemed to be suitable for mating with females or for sperm removal. They possessed various traits which might help them survive outside the building. All the bodies of the male specimens were slim and quite muscular but there was a continuous variation among them of skin tone, stature, height and hair texture. The range and gradation of these physical features would describe normal distribution curves had they been plotted out on graph paper. The male torsos were all immersed in the emerald green stasis fluid which nourished their cells and maintained organ function. None of these men had conscious brain functions and they were all recipients of John's neural implants so that he could instruct them as he wished.

In the area to John's right lay the vats of women. Row after row of containers of pink syrup enveloped their nude bodies. They moved around aimlessly in the medium without cognition or conscious thought. Like the men, the females were in good physical shape and came in all racial types and skin colours. Some were flat chested while others were heavy breasted. This was not one of the features deciding their fate. John was interested in their viability for mating and carrying children plus their potential as egg donors.

The small area on the other side of the spherical building was where John stored the children resulting from his research and these were maintained in vats containing an orange viscous medium specially adapted to maintain young tissues and organs. It was the children stored here that gave John his greatest hope of successful human release into the outside world in terms of their survival. The male and female adults stored in this region were 'special' and separate from the main mass of torsos. They were John's 'best' specimens and represented what he called his 'prime group' of subjects for mating, giving birth and removal of reproductive germ cells for genetic engineering purposes. A few of the females were pregnant. The adults had already been genetically modified and stood the greatest chance of survival outside the protective building. There were about thirty men and a similar number of women in stasis in this area. Included in this storage area were a couple of 'extra special' people. These were his old Earth wife Sylvie and his daughter-in-law Jane.

John's experiments were beginning to bear fruit. Ideally, he would have liked to release most of the mass of men and women into the outside Earthly environment beyond the building knowing they had a good chance of survival. Many of this human mass were becoming surplus to his requirements. They had less chance of survival than his collection of genetically modified best specimens in his prime group. He was now seriously considering releasing the bulk of people from their storage vats into the outside environment. He could then monitor them and observe their viability. He would be able to identify whatever harmful effects befell them. After all, he could always time travel back into the past and collect more replacement specimens should some of them die. If he could identify any bodily survival advantages, using this knowledge he might be able to 'tweak' the metabolism of those individuals in his special group to overcome any harmful environmental effects and thus safely release his prime group. This was John's primary aim. He did, however, have an alternative plan should the release of the masses in the vats turn out to be a complete disaster. This second option was a technological answer to once and for all deal with the problems imposed by the harsh planetary environment. It was not so much a cure but an avoidance strategy. This means of survival had been fully prepared by his scientific and engineering predecessors. However, it was much less certain to succeed than the Great Plan for repopulation of the Earth. He would have to try this first before contemplating the more difficult alternative and final option.

John's past meeting with his son Kevin had slightly dented his moral compass. John considered that perhaps he did not have one at all. John mulled over a few scenarios and outcomes in his mind. His mindset was far too advanced along the road of the Great Plan to feel guilt or remorse should it go wrong. However, he did feel a slight reluctance to proceed with his plan. It did occur to him that if things went badly, it would be a great waste of human resources. Although he was not overly stressed about what he planned to do, he knew that his son Kevin would not have approved. John felt his proposed actions were for the greater good. Perhaps his wife Sylvie might also try to turn his mind against his plan if he released her from stasis before he began his next experiment. It would be better to keep Sylvie (and Jane) in storage until such times that even if they tried to influence him on whether to go ahead or not on moral grounds it would be too late. It was time to speed up the Great Plan.

John made his way down a ramp and entered a small side room. He stood opposite the facing wall and after a few moments a bright yellow light filled the room accompanied by a low humming sound. John now needed to focus his thoughts. He was going to transmit instructions to the masses of people in the main storage area. First, he had to remove all the stasis fluid by draining it away through a grid he would open at the base of each vat. Then he would utilise the hoist system to remove all the men and women and stand them outside their vat to await his telepathic instructions. This was to be his greatest day. He hoped all would go well. It would be a risky investigation. Even partial success and survival of some individuals would be enough to allow him to ignore the other less favoured technological option for surviving the future Earth.

It took an hour to drain all the vats and remove the people. The men and women stood motionless in long lines in front of their former vat homes. They stared mindlessly ahead. Soon they would revitalize mentally to the extent that they would be given limited independent thought and actions moderated and controlled by John's thoughts. John completed his mind control instructions and returned to the lofty viewing platform. He could see the large number of naked men and women facing each other, standing silent and still in front of their vats. This would be their last encounter with the stasis containers. Whatever degree of freedom of thought and action was left to them in their life, however limited, it was about to be given to them.

A section of the outer wall of the spherical building 'melted away' leaving an exit route into the outside world. Clothing would not be needed, the temperature was tolerable. There were other environmental hazards that concerned John much more than the temperature. The great release of the abductees would determine their degree of tolerance and longevity in the outside world. John did not expect all the human specimens to survive but he was interested in those who were better adapted and would continue living outside the spherical building. Knowledge of the genetic make up of the survivors would be of great value to him.

The humans paired off. Each male associated with whichever female was opposite and closest. They left the spherical building in two's. It was a scene reminiscent of the animals passing into Noah's Ark two by two. This time naked pairs of men and women were exiting the building in which they had been preserved and kept alive. It was not too clear where they would head for but they remained in the local vicinity of the building in their pairs. The couples began to partake in conversations and they remained calm and collected showing no fear and little curiosity as to their whereabouts. Within forty minutes all the humans were outside the protective building.

Everything went much better than John could have hoped for. The abducted humans exchanged names. They had lost all the other memories of their former lives. The parameters of the conversations were limited. Individuals knew their names but the concept of their childhood history was lost on them. They existed in the 'here and now' and did not contemplate their surroundings. The red sun, blue-green grass and dank air were just there. There was nothing much to think about. No-one was racing off to work, taking holidays or going shopping.

Within ninety minutes of leaving the building the people were mingling and communicating freely. There was no attempt to seek shelter or food. There were no changing weather conditions to cope with. The air was still and the light had a dull reddish hue. John maintained careful observation of the scene. After a few hours, he noted that some of the couples seemed attracted to each other. This was an interesting aspect of his social and survival experiment. In due course, mating occurred. There were no old style social inhibitions about how or where it happened. There were no periods of courting, engagements or marriage. Mating was animalistic in nature. It just happened spontaneously and more or less randomly. Love was an unknown notion to the abductees. John considered that the repopulation project was going to generate its own children without any prompting from him. All was going well.

CHAPTER 3

Find a Partner and Hold Hands

John was pleased that the Great Plan had reached the 'Release' stage of his experimentation. There were about five thousand people in couples standing in the area in front of the exit region of the spherical building. The couples did not wander far away. Once they were outside the building they stood in their pairs talking. Many of the males and females were holding hands. The others stood closely next to each other. The couples were able to continue long lasting trivial conversations without becoming bored with the topic under discussion or with their partner in general. Every now and again a couple would break off from talking, have sexual intercourse and then continue with their robotic conversations.

The conversations were shallow. There were no intellectual or philosophical discussions. The talk centred around commenting on each other's bodies, the spherical building and the external view of the flat blue-green landscape and dull red sun. Even these discourses were short lived. The conversational exchanges did not include discussion of the future prospects for their lives. The couples did not even discuss where they would obtain their food and drink.

John was able to inhibit some brain centres and stimulate others. Many association centres were free to work relatively normally. These included the speech and auditory centres plus the visual cortex which received the final inputs from the optic nerves. Brain areas like the cerebellum were free to carry out their balancing and co-ordination functions while the sleep centre was turned off, at least for the time being. The motor nerves descending from the motor cortex to the body muscles controlling voluntary movement were partially free to operate independently but could be inhibited to prevent the subject from wandering off too far. The sensory cortex of the brain which received inputs from various sensory receptors in the body (including those from the skin's touch and thermo-receptors) was working quite independently. John was keen to monitor autonomic nerve activity and see what happened to physiological factors such as heart rate, breathing and blood pressure in his human guinea pigs. The hindbrain's medulla oblongata controlled blood pressure, heart rate and breathing and it was important to see if this area's functions could be maintained for long periods in the outside environment. John had a firm grip on memory recall and he could also stimulate parts of the brain to initiate thoughts and control locomotion. There was no question of the abductees dissenting from the Great Plan.

It was time to get the people outside the building ready for the forthcoming 'solar event' as they needed to be prepared. John had calculated that the next showing of a solar event would happen within the next three days. The cycle was fairly constant and it was nearly three weeks since the last appearance. In order to gauge the survival qualities of the old Earth humans, it would be best if they were in their peak physical condition possible. John estimated that about thirty percent of the humans liberated into the outside environment would come through the event unscathed. He would then be able to study the genetic constitutions of these survivors. This would help his investigations involving manipulating the human genome. The extra knowledge he would obtain from the survivors of the solar event would allow him to use gene therapy techniques. By splicing DNA, he hoped to be able to produce better quality hybrid children in his prime human stock. These children could become the true long term rulers and replacement population of the future Earth. The people outside the building were simply 'study fodder'. Their numbers could always be added to by collecting more specimens from the past and these would be more grist to the mill. The long term prognosis for many of the current crop of humans standing on the blue-green grass under the red sun was in doubt but those that did survive the coming event would contribute to the future by means of the DNA making up their genes.

The mass of adult couples outside the spherical building needed final preparation and it was time to get started. Not all the people would survive the coming solar event but those that did had to be kept alive for as long as possible. The ones surviving the longest and perhaps even their offspring would provide John with all the genetic knowledge he would need to finally produce a viable gene pool for his prime batch of individuals. This would enable them to recolonize the outside world. This would be the final culmination of the Great Plan.

The five thousand or so people formed up in their pairs so that a long queue formed. It was as if they were waiting in an orderly line for a bus to arrive though no such vehicle was on its way. The queue began walking rather slowly in the reduced gravity around the large spherical building's circumference. The scene was very reminiscent of a school day trip. A long queue of people walked in two's, no longer talking but holding hands, towards the opposite side of the building.

The paired off adults would have made a great sight for old style Earth's equal opportunity rights supporters and those seeking racial and social equality. There were fine haired blonde and pale skinned Caucasian men paired off and holding hands with black women with curly frizzy hair. Sub-continental brown skinned men with black hair walked with their oriental lady partners. Aboriginals were paired with blue eyed blondes. It was a sight equality workers of the past could only have dreamed about.

When all the couples had made the journey round the building they stood in their pairs in a long line, shoulder to shoulder. Opposite and in front of them was a long, grey, pipe-like tube which ran the length of the human chain but originated from inside the spherical building. This long tube resembled old fashioned house guttering and contained flowing medicated and recycled drinking water. The tube was sited about head high off the ground and finger pressure on blue squared areas scattered along the tubing would cause the emission of a small fountain of water fit for drinking and bodily hydration. Underneath the pipe and out of the way of the water fountain vents was a long flat tray made of transparent material. This tray was filled with small multi-coloured 'pills' which closely resembled a popular old Earth confectionary product called 'Smarties' except that these pills were condensed nutritional products containing all the component nutrients, minerals and vitamins required for a balanced diet. Located behind the backs of the people in the long human train was an equally lengthy row of toileting devices designed to withdraw and either destroy or recycle human liquid and semi-solid wastes. There was no shyness or privacy built into the toiletry design for the people, everything was structured towards the need for efficient functionality. The people had all of their cerebral conceptions of shyness or embarrassment deleted from their emotional repertoire so there was no requirement to cater for modesty.

On reduction of the degree of inhibitory stimulation, the human couples re-assumed a near normal lifestyle. The focus of attention as far as conversation was concerned concentrated on the partner of the opposite sex with only limited discourse with nearby couples. The males and females made free use of the food pills and drinking water facilities without considering where these came from or who was supplying them. When the need to pass human waste came upon them, the task was done in a very matter-of-fact way with no more importance than the turning on of a light switch or opening a fridge door.

The crowd of people did not stray any distance from the long grey pipe and were always within view of the spherical building. There was an atmosphere of a well behaved sports crowd quietly chatting before a tennis match. Sometimes the people would stand up and other times sit down on the blue-green grass or just squat. One or two individuals even lay prone on their backs facing upwards to the black sky and red sun. There were of course no packets of popcorn, no hot dogs and no cans of coke. The people were waiting for an event to occur but they did not know this. Perhaps had they known about it, they would not have remained in such a calm and relaxed frame of mind.

John was very content at this point. The five thousand or so human subjects were all behaving correctly. They were eating, drinking and mating. Their thoughts could be monitored and their movements controlled. The DNA of those who came through the event would give him the final key to unlock the door of long term survival on the planet. He expected a fair proportion of the human throng to come through the event relatively unscathed. The people were physically fit and their minds were not troubled by extraneous events which might distract them. Even if just a small percentage of the group remained alive and well after the event was over, it would be fine.

John's thoughts briefly wandered to his wife Sylvie and daughter-in-law Jane still immersed in the stasis vats along with the other prime human subjects. He hoped he could reactivate and protect them so they could begin to rebuild society on the Earth. It would be nice to converse with his wife again and get to know his daughter-in-law. He was extremely confident all would go well and the Great Plan would soon be another step nearer completion. If it did go badly wrong the Great Plan might have to be abandoned but this was unthinkable. The alternative escape plan was all set up and ready to go but this was only to be undertaken if the worst scenario resulted.

The time passed and on the third day the solar event began as predicted.

CHAPTER 4

The Event

The sun of the future Earth was an 'old lady' but life continued to beat within her breast. She was not done quite yet. Signs of flickering life could be observed on a regular basis. Still, if she was going to die she would take her Earthly neighbours with her. She had spent much of her existence nurturing terrestrial life but if she was going to be extinguished she would not go to her final destiny alone. Her bursts of solar activity were acting as the final slayer of the last vestiges of human evolution.

There was still a photosphere surrounding the 'old lady' but her brightness was severely reduced compared to her younger days. In the old days, her light and heat had sustained all kinds of microbial, plant and animal life. The sun was nearing her death bed. She valiantly fought on and still managed to drag some energy surges from her core. These efforts had sadly hastened the demise of humankind to the point that even after man's selective breeding experiments and genetic reprogramming of individuals only a lone survivor remained. John was determined to beat the odds and resist the deadly discharges which flew across space from the red orb to his treasured planet Earth.

The surface of the future sun had many relatively quiet areas but there were also some active regions which generated solar phenomena. The polar regions of the sun generated solar wind. The solar wind itself consisted of a plasma stream in the upper atmosphere containing charged atomic particles such as protons and electrons. The stream of particles escaped the sun's gravity because of their high energy and travelled to far distant destinations including the heliosphere, a region of space dominated by the sun. The edge of the heliosphere formed a magnetized 'bubble-like medium' stretching far beyond the outer planets of the solar system including Pluto. This bubble was maintained by the plasma of the solar wind.

The solar wind moved at a supersonic speed towards the Earth and caused spectacular light shows in the ionosphere. These were observable on the Earth as the aurorae and geomagnetic storms. The *aurora borealis* (northern lights) and *aurora australis* (southern lights) resulted from the stream of charged particles reaching the planet. Bright auroras had strongly heated the ionosphere in the Earth's atmosphere. Plasma derived from the ionosphere had expanded into the magnetosphere. If a planet has a weak or non-existent magnetosphere it is subject to having its atmosphere stripped away into outer space by the solar wind. There had indeed been a gradual escape of atmospheric contents from the future Earth into space with the solar wind.

Some of the emitted solar charged particles were trapped in a region of space known as the Van Allen radiation belt. The old Earth had always largely been protected from the solar wind by its magnetic field which deflected most of the charged particles. John knew that things had changed in his future Earth. The magnetosphere was considerably reduced and the inhabitants, including John's peers, had suffered the inevitable consequences.

A dark area appeared amid the redness of the overhead orb. John knew that the latest 'event' was starting. The magnetic flux pushed upwards through the photosphere. The cooler plasma below was consequently exposed. The contrast between the photosphere and the solar interior now gave the impression of a dark sunspot. The appearance of this and the follow-on changes would result in human fatalities. John expected the survival of a substantial number of the human abductees located outside the spherical building but a number might perish. They would give John the final genetic data he needed to work with on his group of prime subjects still encased in stasis vats located in the spherical building safely hidden from solar exposure. Their liberation into the future Earth depended on the effects of the solar event on the abductees and his studies of the survivors.

The solar atmosphere was far different in nature and extent compared to what had once been the case. The sunspot grew to a gigantic size visible to the naked eye. The humans outside the spherical building now were induced by John to stand in a long chain adjacent to each other. Their heads were tilted upwards at the red globe and all conversation ceased. It was important that they all had their eyes wide open as John wanted to check for any effects of the solar event on the fundus, the back layer of tissue including the retina within the eye. The humans spread their legs apart to ensure the solar emissions reached the greatest surface area and all parts of the body including the gonads. It was important that the sex organs were fully exposed to the solar activity as any genetic mutations or other changes in the DNA of the sperms and eggs would have to be monitored. The people raised their arms and spread them apart as if showering in a flowing stream of water. John wanted the maximum surface area of skin to be exposed to whatever solar emissions the ageing sun would discharge.

The huge sunspot started to exert its effects. The localised magnetic field became very concentrated in the vicinity of the sunspot. The solar convection currents began to reduce compared to the surrounding photosphere. The surface temperature began to decrease within the dark area and was in sharp contrast to the surrounding material to the extent of about a thousand degrees Centigrade reduction. The luminance was clearly observable against the relative brightness of the surrounding areas. The sunspot had emerged onto the solar photosphere with a diameter of ten miles and moved at a speed of hundreds of miles per second. It rapidly expanded to one hundred thousand miles in diameter and was still growing. The intense magnetic activity of the sunspot generated secondary phenomena which John was expecting. Among these were coronal loops or prominences, coronal mass ejections and solar flares.

The coronal loops connected areas of opposite magnetic polarity in the photosphere of the sun. They were highly structured in nature in the lower transitional region around the sun. Their magnetic flux protruded into the atmospheric corona. Combinations of cool, warm and hot loops radiated energy.

John observed the long chain of humans. They were five thousand enforced 'sun-worshippers'. They were sunbathers exposed to the solar activity unknowingly and without conscious willpower. At one time many years in the past, people had clamoured to find space on crowded sandy beaches to reap the benefits of healthy solar exposure. The skin reacted by making vitamin D and tanned nicely. The sunbathers of old covered their skin with protective sunscreen creams to prevent damage caused by ultraviolet light. Of course, long term exposure to the sun could cause skin carcinomas as well as wrinkling and ageing of the skin. The old sun could easily burn and redden the skin and the eyes were often shaded from the aerial glowing yellow orb. She demanded respect. The future sun was a different protagonist. John was very interested to see how well the abducted sunbathers fared.

The solar event was now well underway and the sun continued to produce her dying tricks. How many would survive?

The solar corona, an outer layer of the sun, released a coronal mass ejection. This took the form of a massive release of gas and an outflux of a magnetic field which further contributed to the solar wind. In the past similar events had taken place but this time the occurrence lasted longer and had a greater magnitude.

The coronal mass ejection threw out a huge amount of matter and electromagnetic radiation into space. This violently ejected plasma disturbed the sun's magnetic field. Initially a 'solar prominence' occurred in the corona but then rapidly spread between and beyond the planets. Part of the ejected material was directed towards the Earth and the solar energetic particles caused atmospheric geomagnetic storms. Particularly strong aurorae became visible around the Earth's magnetic poles. As for the sunbathing humans, they would shortly be exposed to high intensity cosmic rays and charged particles. John was fascinated to find out their effects on survival and if any genetic outrages would occur.

Previous solar activity had devastated the future Earth and not only mankind but life on the Earth in general had suffered. There was no protection against the new incoming waves and particles. Life can only survive within a narrow range of parameters such as temperature, humidity and light intensity. There are optimal conditions for bodily survival but in general conditions need to remain in a state of homeostatic constancy. Living organisms cannot survive outside a narrow deviation of environmental conditions. The gradual loss of an atmosphere made for a pessimistic survival prognosis due to penetrative invasions of dangerous inputs from space. John and his colleagues had tried very hard to overcome the adversity of the changing Earth and had met with some success but things began to get worse with the advent of the solar flares with their increasing frequency and magnitude.

The changing activity of solar flares was revealed to John and his scientific colleagues (when they were still alive) by sudden flashes of brightness over the sun's surface and enlarged sunspots. The movements of charged particles accelerated and generated colossal coronal mass ejections. It only took a short time for the sun's emissions to bathe the Earth. The solar flares were powered by the release of magnetic energy stored in the sun's corona. The heated plasma not only contained charged atomic particles but also a range of electromagnetic radiations including radio waves, X-rays, ultraviolet radiation and gamma rays. An unprecedented high magnitude output of this unhealthy cocktail was heading across space straight towards the humans who stood with open eyes and splayed limbs before the red orb's latest solar event.

CHAPTER 5

Cosmic Tanning

The health threat posed by the incoming solar discharge (and also galactic cosmic rays) could result in a range of diseases if not fatality in humans on the Earth's surface exposed to the assault. However, some individuals might have eyes more resistant to damage than others, skin that could resist radiation or be less prone to malignancies and so on. John needed to locate and isolate those genes with good survival value from his human specimens. He could then utilise the DNA of such genes by making genetic incisions and splicing the beneficial genes into hybrid children of his prime group of specimens still stored in the stasis vats. Even better, he could utilise mating or *in vitro* fertilizations such that he could give gene therapy to unborn embryos. He would have to exclude the genes identified with less suitable DNA for survival from these embryos. The individuals that perished as a result of exposure to the solar activity would enable John to identify, locate and isolate undesirable genetic fragments. On the other hand, the survivors of the harsh exposure would allow him to move his research forwards by letting him identify and select useful genes which could be added to the embryos genetic constitution.

The solar particles reaching the Earth consisted mainly of protons. These were energetically accelerated by the sun.

This was related to their proximity to the solar flares and coronal mass ejection. Incoming cosmic rays reaching the Earth from deep space were mainly composed of high energy protons, helium and some other high energy ions (charged atoms). These emissions represented potential acute and chronic causes of health risks and their effects were likely to be exacerbated by the Earth's thinned atmosphere and reduction of its ozone layer.

The exposed humans might be affected immediately by the incoming bombardment or more gradually over time. John intended to investigate any damage done to human DNA by such incoming radiations from space. As yet unknown acute and quick appearing harmful radiation effects might occur in some humans following the solar particle event due to the high radiation dose emitted on the current occasion. Another possibility was that exposure would encourage chronic and long term serious health problems such as carcinoma tumour formation or degenerative effects on body tissues. Other effects of the radiation might be less serious and one problem John anticipated might occur was ocular damage and cataract formation. The photoreceptors in the retina of the eye were also at high risk due to ion absorption in the viscous vitreous humour in the posterior region of the eye. The humans exposed in the unshielded environment outside the spherical building would receive doses of radiation more than a thousand times of that on the old Earth.

Many cells in the people exposed to the emissions of high energy particles were likely to die due to deleterious short and long term effects on their central nervous systems. This was another area that John needed to investigate. He intended to examine and monitor the survivors to find out what genetic or other factors had kept their nerve cells functioning normally. There was a definite risk to cells in various vital brain centres which might not only shorten life span but terminate it forthwith. In the long term John believed that even many survivors of the solar exposure event would run the risk of accelerated onset of Alzheimer's disease and other brain dysfunctions. John was very aware that exposure of surface dwelling humans to solar outrages on the future Earth would not be a one off occurrence. The solar events were ongoing and repeating hence there would be cumulative damaging effects on the body with increasing exposures.

The radiation levels found in deep space were very unlike those on the old Earth's surface. The solar system had always been exposed to high energy galactic cosmic rays, radiation belts and proton radiation from solar events such as flares, mass ejections and the solar wind. The Van Allen radiation belts trapped particles from the solar wind which would accelerate when interacting with the magnetic field of the Earth. The radiation dose had always had the potential to rise even on the old Earth during geomagnetic storms and periods of increased solar activity. However, without shielding on the future Earth, acute radiation sickness and death had become more serious threats than in days gone by. The ongoing increases in emissions reaching the Earth's surface represented a challenge to John's ingenuity in enabling human existence to continue unscathed on the planet.

John was extremely confident that the Great Plan would succeed and allow him to accomplish his goal of reinstating mankind as the species which would dominate and be master of the Earth. All aspects of the plan were in operation and his research on the survivors of the solar event would almost guarantee the success of his mission. There was a contingency plan if things went wrong but this would be the last resort.

John's now dead colleagues had considered the possibility of building sub-surface cities to protect the population but the mantle and crust were subject to instability and the idea was eventually abandoned. Consideration had been given to constructing numerous large buildings to shelter the human population. It was deemed that these would become overcrowded with time and the synthetic materials required for construction were too limited in supply with respect to the quantities needed to make the plan feasible. The best solution to the increasingly hostile terrestrial conditions was the Great Plan. However, the scientific community had not anticipated that the conditions on the Earth would deteriorate so quickly due to the ever changing solar cycles. These harsh changes had caused quick, and numerous fatalities within the human population and mankind had been taken to the brink of extinction. Should John not be able to complete his survival programme he still had one 'ace up his sleeve' but it was not what he currently had in mind and one which his dead peers found undesirable.

In the past the Earth's upper atmosphere had blocked deep intrusion of primary cosmic rays from space. Some secondary radiation was absorbed in the atmosphere before it reached the surface of the planet and the bombarding particles decayed on this journey into fundamental subatomic particles such as muons and pions. Atmospheric shielding had historically been the key to the safety of life and survival on the Earth. Although the radiation dose was usually higher at the poles compared to the equator, the levels had always been within survival range. Gyrations of the magnetic field of the old Earth ensured that harmful cosmic rays were deflected away.

In the future Earth there had developed an urgent need to be shielded against the heightened exposure to charged particles and cosmic rays. It had not proved possible to build underground cities or sufficient numbers of big enough buildings to provide shelter. Therefore, it was essential that John complete his mission of modifying the human body to allow it to survive the new harsh conditions. The only other choice was to escape from the Earth completely.

John observed the external scene from within the 'safe zone' of the spherical building. Naked humans stood outside exposed to all of the incoming radiation. He would now disengage the human guinea pigs from some of his direct thought intervention, at least for the time being. The solar event was over and now it was time to observe and study the effects of the exposure. How would the bodies of the people react? The humans would be allowed to mingle and communicate with each other while being kept in the vicinity of the spherical building and within his field of view.

John had ensured that the minds of the human subjects were inhibited as far as emotions were concerned. If some of the people died it would not suit the programme of the Great Plan for others to show grief. He was in need of those dead bodies to check their 'weak' genetic traits that had allowed them to die. This would involve both autopsies of the dead bodies, microscopic examination of the tissues and biochemical analysis of the DNA. The living peers of any departed individuals would be made to bring the dead bodies to the entrance of the building where he would deal with them. Those people would then have to return to and socialise with the rest of the survivors.

John decided it was time for some contemplation. He suspected that some mal-effects of solar exposure might show within twenty four hours. However, most short term health issues within the group due to particle and cosmic ray exposure would most likely manifest during the coming week. Any long term damage to the people in the study group might not matter so much. He hoped to have solved the problem of survival and implement a solution in the prime group of people still safe in the storage vats before any long term damage showed up in the survivors.

John had some technological means at his disposal for counteracting the harmful solar surges but these were minimal and mainly employed within the spherical building. They could not be used outdoors. The rapid increases in deleterious solar activity had caught the scientists and engineers on the future Earth 'on the hop' and they did not have enough time to develop protective measures *en masse*. John hoped he could maintain and extend the life of those individuals currently still in stasis.

John looked across the open spaces, floors and ramps of the spherical building. The storage vats were empty, except for those of his prime group of people. He had made so many time jumps to collect the best human specimens and bring them to this place. The range of human types he had managed to abduct indicated that he had done a good job of collecting specimens with an excellent range of genetic diversity. The large rectangular surgical theatre like rooms had been well equipped by his forerunners. Time portal technology had ensured that a supply of new human bio-material was always available.

Far back in history, scientists had uncovered the secrets of subatomic particle physics. Discoveries and inventions followed one after the other and within a relatively short time technologies had developed such as time portals and star gates. Exotic propulsion systems had also become commonplace including star ship drives and antigravity technology. Once it became known how to utilise wormholes and warp spacetime, human existence reached a new level of exploration. This was accompanied by an increase in spirituality and changes to the values of human society. However, a drop in emotional attachments and concern for others made human inter-relationships much less tight. This was the area in which John had come into conflict with the views of his son Kevin during their temporal encounter. John had discovered some residual emotions within himself. Although he had genetically altered Amy, John had allowed Kevin's daughter to remain with him on the old Earth in the past and thus avoid her planned further participation in the Great Plan. However, John had continued with his human collection and storage programme and was ruthlessly engaged upon studying the environmental effects on the released subjects. The Earth remained the birthplace of humanity and abandoning her to her fate without the presence of any human life on it was a last and permanent resort.

John was neither 'evil' nor callous. His mind worked differently to the people from the old Earth. When a bulldozer digs a trench in the ground and dislodges and maims thousands of earthworms, does the driver go to bed at night worrying about his daily activities? When a housewife sprays her lounge with fly killer and the flies drop dead in agony, does she suffer pangs of conscience? The answer of course is 'no' and this reflected John's outlook. He patiently waited for any effects on his human subjects exposed to the environmental radiation to show.

John made a visit to the storage vats where the prime group of people in stasis were located. It would be nice should it prove possible to liberate his wife Sylvie and daughter-in-law Jane. He would find a way of supporting their survival. Perhaps Jane could be restored to her husband Kevin and their daughter Amy in the past on the old Earth. A lot depended on the outcome of his experiment on survival to the solar event.

John's considerations of long term health issues relating to solar exposure would require monitoring any occurrences of carcinogenic tumours, ocular problems, behavioural changes or nervous damage. However, in the first instance he was mainly interested in the short term survival of his radiation exposed human collection as he needed to know the acute effects on the body. If he could find a swift genetic answer which could beat the problems caused by irradiation he would not need to worry about long term problems.

John decided it was time to return to the viewing position to observe the external crowd. He would look for any early signs of poor health before physically going among the survivors to start initial genetic monitoring. He reached the viewing platform and peered at the scene spread out before him.

Had John been subject to old fashioned human emotions, he would at this point have been experiencing these in bountiful supply. As it was, he surveyed a scene of desolation. Although a human tragedy was in full view, to John it was merely a totally unexpected experimental observation. He surveyed the scene not with compassion or grief but with surprise. 'Shock' would be too strong a sentiment but his mind was filled with disbelief. Outside the spherical building about half the humans lay prone. They were already dead. Their bodies were twisted from their agonising death throes and their faces were twisted in death masks of pain.

The people that were still alive were in various parlous states. Some lay on the ground writhing in agony. Others staggered aimlessly around, tripping over dead bodies, getting up only to fall again. A few sat on their haunches head lowered between their knees, vomiting and helplessly suffering episodes of diarrhoea. Their exposed skin had extensive patches of purpura, red and purple regions that were unaffected by any attempt to rub and soothe them. All five thousand of his human experimental subjects would shortly be dead. The solar exposure experiment of the Great Plan had not worked.

John needed to understand what had happened. He had to make an assessment of the situation and a reasoned judgement. The increase in solar activity had caught John out in his projected outcome. The extent of exposure of the human bodies to the ionizing solar particles and cosmic rays had been outrageous and underestimated. It seemed as if the sun had taken on John in a personal duel.

John had considered that short term radiation poisoning

might have caused death in some individuals between three to thirty days or so following exposure but the situation in front of him was far worse than he had contemplated. An initial autopsy of a few sample corpses showed a catastrophic loss of cells in the bone marrow required for vital new blood cell formation. There was also extensive damage to the cells in the wall of the small intestine. The finger-like microvilli needed for absorbing nourishment and transferring it from the gut into the bloodstream had degenerated. Vital organs had been starved of their nutrients.

The cadavers began to reveal their deathly secrets to John's probes and analysers. The ability of cells to undergo mitosis had been severely reduced. Without this cell division, the processes of growth and tissue repair could not continue. Analysis of the pitiful souls still alive showed that their DNA was damaged and the symptoms they were displaying were a prelude to death. John could not help any of them. It was very disappointing because he had wished to clone or replicate the DNA of survivors that could resist the detrimental environment outside the shielded spherical building. It was apparent that the solar barrage outside the building had now reached a level far beyond the durability of human life.

The humans that were still alive were now demonstrating various further gastrointestinal defects including nausea and vomiting. As their blood count fell, anaemia and internal bleeding also began. Neurological exposure ensured that there was a regular occurrence of further deaths. Even if it had been possible for some individuals to have survived the solar event, in the longer term they would probably have succumbed to a variety of cancers. However, the possibility of any survivors being alive beyond the next twenty four hours was close to nil.

The exposure to a massive dose of radiation had caused the rapid onset of symptoms leading to fatality. This was made worse by whole body exposure to the solar outrage. John had directed his human subjects to stretch their naked bodies out for maximal surface exposure of their human tissues to the sun's emanations. They had no chance of remaining alive.

John returned to his viewing station some hours later. There were still about fifty people alive but barely so. They now expressed a very wide range of nasty symptoms. He made a mental note of their induced dysfunctions. The number of radiation sickness indications was extensive. He now observed individuals with an even wider range of symptoms adding to what he had already observed. On this viewing he found the human victims not only presenting with nausea, vomiting, raised body temperature, reddened skin and fatigued muscles but also confusion, dizziness, headaches, convulsions and abdominal pains. The dwindling number of survivors felt no semblance of any drive to eat or drink and most had uncontrolled diarrhoea. Other unpleasant bodily functions also afflicted a few people including epilation (hair loss) and hypotension (low blood pressure). The symptoms would very soon be followed by shock and death.

CHAPTER 6

May Your Genes Protect You: DNA to Die For

The research and technological efforts to repopulate the future Earth had been enormous. Studies and projects had continued for several generations. Even though the technologies in use were far in advance of those understandable in current times, the malfunctioning sun was a daunting challenge and beyond what even futuristic *Homo sapiens futuralis* humans could control. The sun had been in a metamorphosis for millennia but when the process sped up, human survival time was limited. The Great Plan had been drawn up by the best scientific minds of the time and had widespread support.

Some way had to be found to survive the sun's increasingly harmful emissions. There were not enough materials in abundance to consider hiding from the solar emissions below ground in underground cities or for constructing enough safe buildings. The spherical building was the only shielded structure to have been completed.

The future Earth's scientists had solved many of the problems, issues and conundrums facing current day physicists. Many years had passed since a comprehensive understanding of fundamental subatomic particles had been obtained. The ramifications of this knowledge had been enormous. A great range of new technologies came into being which previously could only have been dreamed about. The way the Universe worked, its nature and its natural laws had become opened up to human exploitation. Theories such as had been proposed in ancient times by people such as Einstein and his ideas of Special Relativity were made use of in ways not foreseen by present day scientists. No longer was the speed of light a restriction on how fast an object could travel. Close to light speed propulsion systems were commonplace and it was also possible to bend spacetime so achieving incredible warp drive engines.

The understanding of the slowing down of time as the speed of light was approached led to scientists developing exotic technologies which were able to warp spacetime such that time and dimensional jumps through portals had become a reality. It was only possible to move a small amount of matter through them on any one occasion of use due to the huge energy requirement required for them to work. If more than one person intended to traverse a quantum field change or warp the fabric of spacetime in a leap through time only one person at a time could enter the time and distance spatial distortion provided by the time warp devices.

Human population numbers outside the spherical building had dropped year by year. For a long time there had been an increasing annual mortality rate. The sun slowly became more and more harmful. Scientists struggled to keep up with the changing sun and its malevolent outbursts by tweaking the physical and metabolic features of newborn infants. It was barely possible for this gene therapy to compensate for the increased severity and range of health problems posed by the changing solar activity. Eventually, things had come to the point where those dwelling outside the protective environment of the spherical building perished after any considerable period of solar exposure. Only a selected elite group of individuals including John had been chosen to retreat into the bowels of the building to continue the Great Plan. Even these people of great intellect had not foreseen the sudden increasing vehemence of the sun's anger that would befall planet Earth in due course.

Time passed and the elite group of people toiled hard to find a way to discover a mode of survival outdoors. The biochemists, physiologists and medics combined their expertise to produce the medium used in the storage vats. They discovered a fluid medium which could maintain the life of a human body in a suspended form of existence which became known as stasis. This might have been called suspended animation in the old days but the process was quite different. In fact, the animation of the body could continue almost indefinitely while the body was immersed in the viscous life sustaining medium. Experiments resulted in minor variations in the constituency of the stasis medium being concocted for use with males, females or children. Engineers quickly developed a working design of container they termed vats in everyday language which would fully immerse people in the stasis medium. It was unsure how long people could be healthily maintained within the storage vats but many scientists including John believed that safe storage would be possible for many human life spans. The mind of those immersed in the vats had to be inactivated while in such storage but this was no problem since implant technology and/or intense telepathic instruction could reactivate nervous pathways and cerebral awareness on release.

The mainly scientific, medical/biotechnological and engineering population within the spherical building began to age and die. Previous exposures to the sun's radiations had induced cancers and other diseases even in those now inside the safe haven. The responsibility had eventually fallen on John alone to complete the Great Plan. He was the only survivor of futuristic mankind. *Homo sapiens futuralis* was on the brink of following the *Dodo* and other species into oblivion by way of extinction.

John now took some time out from the situation he was faced with as the sole survivor of the group of people who confidently had planned to spread mankind across the terrestrial globe just as it had been in the old days. He was the only person who could find a way of saving humankind from extinction. Even John's futuristic brain and enhanced faculties required a few moments distraction away from studying the cause of human deaths and genetic research. He briefly cleared his mind of his task and the delivery of the Great Plan and reflected on his own life. What were the significant events of his life? How might his life have been different without the solar destruction visited on life in his current future Earth? Who had he valued as people during his lifetime other than his peers and colleagues? In a rare few moments of lateral thought, John reflected on family matters especially relating to his wife, son, daughter-in-law and granddaughter. His mind briefly wandered over historical events. He mulled over many things in his memories that he rarely accessed and gave himself permission to think about the background to his current situation.

John's reflections moved to his use of the time portal technology. During one of his time jumps back to the old Earth, he had met Sylvie. She was initially just one of the Great Plan's human subjects ripe for abduction but somehow a great rapport emerged between them. John surprised himself and married Sylvie in an old Earth ceremony. Back in his future time, his wife Sylvie was now maintained in a storage vat in stasis on the future Earth along with other members of the prime group of humans. Throughout her life on the old Earth, Sylvie never spoke to anyone about her futuristic husband or the knowledge she had gained from him. John considered this to be admirable and a great show of loyalty to him.

John then remembered how he had struggled with the idea of having a child with a woman from a past era. His passion had overwhelmed him and this was totally unlike him and something unexpected of himself. However, when Sylvie announced she was pregnant he felt great joy in the concept of having an offspring. John and Sylvie in due course had a son who used the name Kevin Powell while he was with his mother on the old Earth. John had inserted an implant into his son to ensure that he could download information into his mind and control him should it become necessary. He allowed Kevin to spend his childhood on the old Earth. Kevin's memories started at the age of eight when he first began to experience some strange scenarios that he did not understand. They were in fact images and thoughts relating to Earth's future that entered his mind via the implant in his neural tissue either directly from its programming or induced by his father's thought power. John's thoughts at this point were akin to day dreaming. At least he did not have to think about death, genetic manipulation and his strategies for survival, at least for a short while.

Kevin had matured on the old Earth into an adult and in turn had married his beloved girlfriend Jane. Their daily life on the old Earth was very 'normal' and they were both employed. As had happened in his childhood, an adult Kevin again experienced some bizarre events which he did not know were induced by his father. He had experienced views of the future Earth without full comprehension of the significance. Jane had become pregnant and along with husband Kevin had been brought into the future world by John. She gave birth to daughter Amy who quickly was given an implant device by her father Kevin under the influence of John. John then ensured that his daughter-in-law Jane was placed in a vat where she remained safely in stasis near to John's wife Sylvie among the prime group of humans. John now considered his options for the future lives of his family members. The responsibility for their welfare was down to him alone. John's mind continued to wander, reflecting on his experiences.

John had been pleased with his son's choice of female partner for his wife in picking Jane. She was attractive and had a good genetic pedigree. He also had great affection for his granddaughter Amy. He was so proud of her. John reflected on the great plans he once had for his granddaughter. He had hoped that Amy would fulfil her destiny as a major cog in the wheel of the Great Plan to repopulate the Earth in his future time zone. John had undertaken some genetic manipulations on her related to her potential survival on the future Earth. After some time in storage in a stasis container, John returned young Amy to her father Kevin on the old Earth. He did this when she physically attained the age of eight.

John's plan was that Amy would be returned to the past where she had been conceived and would be allowed to spend her remaining childhood development under the care of her dad Kevin. This would continue until Amy attained a stage of physical maturity at which point he would require her for his repopulation programme. At that point she would have to return to the future and would have her previous memories erased. John felt proud that his own granddaughter might possess the correct combination of genes to ensure that mankind had a future. John continued to reflect on his life and evaluated his assessment of Amy's potential as a source of resistant genes.

Kevin loved his daughter very dearly. He was made aware of the predicament of the future Earth and the crucial role of his dad in attempting to re-establish a human population. However, Kevin tried hard to resist the intention of his father to take Amy back into the future and fought him mentally to allow her to stay where she was and live out her life on the old Earth in peace. At one point Kevin thought he had won the power struggle with John and that his love for his daughter had overcome the wishes and plans of his father. Unfortunately, the influence of the neural implant in Kevin was irresistible and Kevin realised that there was nothing he could do to prevent his dad's planned destiny for Amy occurring. Kevin had more or less given up his ethical arguments with his dad to leave Amy where she was. She was a beautiful bright young lady not a laboratory rat bred for experimentation.

John had proved to be very stubborn. He was apparently beyond influence. Then a 'miracle' happened. Suddenly and unexpectedly, John relented. This went against all of John's futuristic instincts. All his efforts directed towards the execution of the Great Plan were put to one side. John decided to allow his son Kevin to continue to interact in the life of his daughter Amy who would be allowed to continue her life on the old Earth. Kevin respected his dad for taking such a hard decision.

John would need to complete the Great Plan without using his granddaughter as a living test animal. John reflected on this humanitarian decision. To him it was the hardest decision of his life. Perhaps his choice of outcome proved that *Homo sapiens futuralis* was still human. Some level of emotional response still existed within his soul. He was pleased to discover he had one.

As John surveyed the scene of decimation he realised that the Great Plan was obsolete. The compelling evidence for this was the five thousand lifeless bodies spread out on the artificial blue-green grass. There was no way humans could survive on this now alien Earth. My goodness, he had tried so hard. Earth would become a barren wilderness left to its own devices, freed at last from the hominid intruder and all the rest of natural animal and plant life. The sun would rule the roost alone in complete mastery of her realm on the Earth. This birthplace of life had run its course. There was no place to hide. The final solution was all that was left. John owed something to those individuals of the prime group who were still in storage vats under his care. The unwanted option left to him was the only action he could now take.

If mankind was no longer welcome on the Earth then the ultimate strategy would have to be undertaken. John was resolved to carry out this final choice despite his reluctance to do so and his disappointment with the demise of the Great Plan. This unhoped for ending was all that was left. It was time to escape from planet Earth and leave her to cope without any natural life to keep her company.

CHAPTER 7

The Space Ark

So far the spherical building had protected the occupants from any harm caused by the excesses of the solar activity. The increasing intensity of solar emissions now had the potential to result in the final extinction of John and the remaining survivors in the stasis tanks. They were unaware of John's failed efforts to find a way of overcoming the environmental changes and repopulating the surface of the Earth. Perhaps it was best they did not know. John considered it wise never to tell them about the deaths of so many human beings in his experiment in which he caused them to expose their naked bodies to the sun's cocktail of emissions outside the relative safety of the spherical building.

John had not expected his son Kevin to raise ethical issues regarding his efforts to give humankind continued existence. John's daughter-in-law Jane had been brought into the future from a past era of human history to give birth there and provide John with access to her offspring. It was likely that she also would not think highly of the destruction of her peers and others from the past resulting from his experimentation on them during the solar event. John did not wish to be in conflict with his daughter-in-law when he released her from stasis.

Even John's wife Sylvie might not approve of his willingness to allow so many people to suffer and die even if it had been done with good intentions. After all, although Sylvie had always been loyal and supportive of John and his plans but like the deceased human guinea pigs, she also originated from a past Earthly historical existence in common with the deceased people who underwent lethal solar power.

John could of course impose his views and limit behavioural responses by utilising telepathic influences on Sylvie and Jane or via the neural implants in other members of the surviving prime group. However, he felt that once the stasis programme was terminated and the vat occupants released, there would be greater long term survival value if he allowed them the scope and freedom to think for themselves and learn to solve their own problems. He could not be relied on forever to be the guardian of their thoughts and actions. Anyway, if the escape plan was to be put into action, the liberated vat occupants and their offspring would ultimately have no choice but to function independently. In the long term future, there was no requirement for him to control their minds or even any necessity for him to communicate with them. John's plan for the ultimate fate of himself and his immediate family did not coalesce with that of the other members of the surviving prime group still in stasis.

John did not regret the five thousand deaths he had caused. He had not set out to purposely cause death. Death was just an unfortunate side effect of the Great Plan to create people who could survive the sun's emissions and start a new civilization outside the spherical building. It still seemed to John that the plan of trying to establish a new human population on the Earth had been the right route to take and outweighed any qualms about individual rights to continue with their old daily lives.

The spherical building still protected the occupants from the sun's radiation. With the surprisingly rapid increase in the severity of the sun's emissions, this might change at any time. John knew he would have to put the final escape option into effect quickly. If he should die and if the members of the remaining prime group of humans were never released from stasis, it would be the final extinction of humankind.

John was very disappointed with the failure of the Great Plan. So much time and effort had been put into bringing suitable human specimens into the future Earth, surgically inserting implants and using their DNA for genetic modification of the human race. John's peers had all now perished but he knew they had relied on him to complete their task. They did not know the plan to genetically manipulate and release a population of solar resistant individuals had not come to successful fruition. John had believed he would succeed but the truth was he was finally beaten. Now he only had the final option at his disposal. He had to face reality.

John stood within the dome in the roof of the spherical building. There was a small concealed control panel which he would soon activate. Once it was activated there was no going back. The control panel would be sealed off by a camouflaged wall covering making it very difficult to be accessed again. He entered a binary code and newly flashing lights on the panel indicated that the pre-set programmes for long term survival by way of escape were installed correctly and ready to run. John double checked the journey co-ordinates. A star map flashed in a 3-dimensional grid above the control panel indicating a galactic route ending at a pre-determined destination. The life and environmental support systems were in order and operative for a long journey. The water recycling system was functional as was the food replicator technology. The waste disposal outlets would become active in a few moments. Medical facilities were available in the large theatre like rooms. The propulsive systems were active and ready to operate.

John's next task was to activate the neural implants to download medical knowledge and instructions for using advanced technological equipment into a few selected people he had chosen from those still in stasis within the storage vats. He set the 'start programme' on a timer with a fifty minute delay. John would have to get a move on now before the escape programme initiated. He wanted to ensure that when the programme started he would be in his correct designated place. The programme would end many years into the future. This would happen when the star map indicated the appropriate position in the cosmos had been reached. At this point Sylvie, Jane and himself would automatically be released from stasis to join any other surviving humans already freed and living in the escape craft.

There was one last general system-check to carry out. If this system broke down trapping him in permanent stasis it could be the end for everybody. The spherical building had done an excellent job protecting its inhabitants from the harmful solar attacks outside its boundary walls. John considered it to be a wise precaution to quickly check that the functionalities of the protective systems were intact. His haste was because overwhelming emissions from the sun reaching the Earth would soon overcome even the defences of the spherical building and the frequency of solar eruptions was increasing. Also, the escape programme was now ticking on a time sensor and the programme would begin whether he was ready or not.

Even in the depths of outer space there were still dangers despite the presence of protective technologies. Cosmic rays, proton and other particles were potential invisible death sentences. The defence systems had to be in good working order. This was vital. Even at distances far away from the sun's influence, radiations still posed a threat. In deep space, the available technology could block completely or reduce them to a non-hazardous intensity. Any exposure to radiation in deep space that did occur would involve only low doses and this would be more manageable and less harmful compared to receiving a single huge exposure from a solar eruption as had recently happened outside the spherical building.

Drugs and medications would be available to combat radiation poisoning but hopefully these would not be required if the protective shielding did its work. There were substances available which enhanced the body's natural defences to repair tissue damage caused by radiation. Vitamin-like compounds in the retinoid family were powerful antioxidants. They inhibited cell division and retarded tumour formation. Their use would ensure that detrimental mutations would not have sufficient time to replicate themselves so the body would be better able to fix damage and repair itself.

John's checks showed that the shielding systems of the spherical building were still operative. The walls of the spherical building were much more technologically complex than might appear with a simple quick observation. Systems were incorporated into the material which produced both magnetic deflection of charged radiation particles and electrostatic repulsion. The former made use of superconductors and plasma currents. The electrostatic shields used powerful accelerator technology. Other measures were also built into the shielding system against charged particles and electromagnetic wave hazards. These included the use of layers of water, liquid hydrogen and aluminium as barriers to prevent harmful penetration and hazardous exposures.

John now activated the implants in the males, females and children still in the storage vats. The prime group of human specimens started to receive downloaded information which would allow them sufficient awareness and familiarity with their surroundings so that on their release they could independently manage daily survival. They received knowledge of how to vent out waste, obtain food and water and were given the psychological freedom to socialise. The individuals given medical expertise would have the skills to mediate health care provision should the need arise. There would be no requirement for navigators or engineers.

In twenty minutes all the stasis vats would be drained and the occupants released. By then the escape sequence would be complete. The occupants would be released and free to roam the building. They would be able to observe outside the spherical building through the viewing dome where John was now standing in the roof. There would be no sign of the control panel as within moments it would be sealed off and hidden. The main restriction on the released occupants would be that there would be no exit system from the building, at least within the foreseeable future. They would be allowed to organise and develop their own social system of hierarchy and family groups.

John had to hurry. He could hear the spherical building humming. There was also a slight vibrating sensation as might be experienced with a minor earth tremor. The instruction sequence was set and the control panel was now hidden away and could not be tampered with. John hurried down the ramp and round the corridors until he entered the room containing the storage vats enclosing Sylvie and Jane. These two family individuals would not share the destiny of the rest of the people in the stasis vats. John had other plans for them. The other vats were beginning to drain away their syrupy liquid contents and the humans within were beginning to regain cognition and freewill. They would soon be released into the spherical building and have to start taking responsibility for their own lives again. They were now 'hard-wired' with survival knowledge via their implant technology and the building would look familiar to them and feel like 'home territory'.

John stood in front of Sylvie and Jane. Their stasis vats were still filled with fluid. They both floated in the supporting medium and their naked bodies gyrated. Arms and legs flailed but no physical damage ensued. The thickness of the fluid medium slowed down their movements and any impact with the vat walls was nullified. Jane's eyes rolled back in their sockets exposing the whites of her eyes. This was normal and her extrinsic ocular eye muscles including the recti and oblique muscles were undamaged. They would be able to regain normal control of her eye movements when she was released from stasis. John's daughter-in-law retained her beauty and youth. Her long blonde hair fluttered with the fluid movements like seaweed wafting in the tide as the sea enters and exits a marine rock pool.

John's loyal wife Sylvie was a more mature figure. She had aged into her sixties when removed from the old Earth but now physically resembled her younger self and looked twenty years more youthful than her biological age. A combination of passing through the time portal technology and the rejuvenation properties of the stasis fluid had returned much of Sylvie's youthfulness to her. Sylvie stared blankly at John but he knew that one day her eyes would focus on him and she would be pleased to see him again.

The passage of time would be meaningless to both Sylvie and Jane. They would in due course regain their old Earth memories. Sylvie would remember her maternal role bringing up Kevin through childhood as the son of John and herself. She would also recall her friendship and bonding with Jane. As well as revealed warm memories of Sylvie, Jane would recall her husband Kevin and regain her feelings of love. Her maternal instincts and memories would also become restored and she would long to see her child Amy. All this was still to come.

The tanks were now draining out the remains of the stasis fluid. The abducted humans would shortly be released and be able to start their new lives. All that remained was for John to complete the final part of the escape plan. He only had a little spare time left. The control panel had been activated to begin the escape procedure in a very short while.

John took one final look around the room. The males were beginning to show signs of awareness and their eyes became more focussed as if they were beginning to observe the nature of the room around them. The emerald green stasis fluid was draining away quickly through the base of their vats and their heads were now exposed to the air. Thoracic respiratory movements were beginning to occur initiated by reflex contractions of the intercostal muscles between the ribs and the diaphragm muscle separating the chest from the abdomen.

The female recovery sequence was taking a slightly different physiological route than that of the men. They were no longer making rotational movements of the torso and the movements of their arms and legs were becoming more co-ordinated and less involuntary. Like the vats containing the men, the fluid stasis medium drained away at an increasing rate and where there had been pink fluid there was now air.

The orange medium containing the hybrid and genetically engineered children had sunk a little lower down into the storage vats. These would take a little longer than the adult vats to drain. The adults would need extra time to orientate themselves and gather their thoughts before the children were released from stasis into their care.

Everything was functioning correctly. The escape event was due to occur just before the final release of the people from the vats. By the time they were free, the escape procedure would be complete and they would be unaware of what had just taken place. They would investigate their surroundings within the spherical building and accept their life there as 'normal existence'. They would quickly get to know their way round the building and understand how everything worked. If they wanted to see outside they could go up to the domed viewing platform in the roof. Friendships and relationships would soon blossom and parental paternal and maternal instincts would quickly 'kick in' to adopt, care for and nurture the children.

John was satisfied that all was well. The escape flight systems were automated and directional instructions for the voyage across space was programmed to run without further input from him. All the survival systems were operative. The prime group of humans would be released from stasis very soon and their functionality restored. They would be freed after the escape from Earth had been completed so they would not be aware of the departure.

John had a few final thoughts about the failure of the Great Plan to repopulate the Earth. It was such a shame that mother Earth would lose her human spawn but it was better to leave her behind and continue the gene pool elsewhere. He still did not regret the deaths of the human guinea pigs in his experiment except in the sense that they had not provided him with the genetic means to repopulate the Earth. He did not have ethical qualms about the deaths though it is fair to say that he would have preferred that no deaths had occurred but he knew it was an inevitable consequence of the experiment.

The humming and vibrating were increasing. John was done. He could now take a long rest. John's telepathic thought power activated the vats containing Sylvie and Jane who were both still completely immersed in the pink stasis fluid. Their two vats moved apart. The gap between the two vats revealed a rectangular space in the floor where the roof of another storage vat sunken below floor level came into view between them. This stasis vat was rapidly filling with emerald green medium. The vats containing Sylvie and Jane on either side of the sunken vat descended downwards below floor level until they stood adjacent to the exposed central vat, one on each side, below the floor. The central vat was now full to the brim with emerald green medium. John was now naked and he slipped his body into the fluid medium through the open top of the middle vat until he was completely immersed. A covering like a lid on a saucepan slid across the top of the vat and sealed him inside. A section of the actual flooring material slid right across the tops of the three sunken vats making them completely invisible from the room containing the storage vats of the other humans making up the prime group. Solid flooring covered over the region where the three vats lay hidden. There was nothing to suggest that three sunken vats were located below the floor. They were completely sealed off.

John had a few moments of cognition left before he lapsed into a stasis trance. He knew that eventually the vats were set to release him automatically from storage in a future time along with Sylvie and Jane. His final conscious moments were spent surveying his surroundings below floor level in a gloomy diffuse light. He took quick sideways glances at Sylvie and Jane in the adjacent vats. They were fine and still supported comfortably within their storage medium. They would be nurtured and sustained as he would also be until the programmed time for release arrived. He peered out of the front of his vat through the casing of the wall. The vats were in a small basement-like space sealed off from the rest of the building above. They would be safe there and undisturbed.

An unknown risk applied at the future date when John, Sylvie and Jane would be released from stasis. At that time the three vats would rise up out of the floor and they would be set free. John did not know how any humans in the building might react when this event occurred. More important was that when they were released, John intended to quickly leave the room currently above them. He planned to lead Sylvie and Jane out of the room and along the exit corridor. A short distance along here was a sealed and disguised entrance to a secret small room better described as a compartment. This space was rather like how many houses have a 'room under the stairs' to store household vacuum cleaners and so on. He hoped nobody would prevent him squeezing into the room with Sylvie and Jane nor did he want other humans forcing an entry into it causing damage to the equipment inside. He did not want the final part of his plan to go wrong. A moment later John's mind was 'gone' and he was in stasis.

The spherical building trembled. The rocky ground below the building crumbled and dust particles blew up into the stale air for the first time in many years. The ceiling material took on a pale yellow incandescent glow which illuminated the internal rooms, corridors and walkways. A shuddering of the complete building heralded its lift off as it hovered over the ground. It remained in this state for over sixty seconds before rising horizontally to the height of a present day skyscraper. Two lower sections surrounding the base of the 'building' began to rotate counter directional to each other. The rotations increased in angular velocity until they were just a blur. A whirring noise filled the air though no-one was there to see or hear the incredible spectacle. The prime group were still in partial stasis at this crucial moment. Below the building where it had been resting on the ground, a large spherical circular region was now visible. The land underneath the building was now bald and there was a complete absence of the artificial blue-green grass. It had been blown and burnt away. Electro-magnetic waves pulsed around the building.

The programmed instructions worked a treat. The spherical building was airborne and hovering horizontally above the Earth. It then tilted to a forty five degrees angle. It continued to hover as if it were surveying the scene. Perhaps the building was paying its final respects to mother Earth. It was as if a son was saying goodbye to his mother knowing that he would never set eyes on her again. There was a resemblance to the old fashioned habit of a man tilting his hat towards a lady being passed by in the street as a polite acknowledgement. Lights flashed around the circumference of the spherical building. It suddenly and without further warning or indication shot silently upwards into the dark sky.

Within a short time the building had cleared the constraints of the Earth's gravity and a blue-green Earth unfamiliar to modern eyes lay far below. The anti-gravity propulsion systems came fully online. The spherical building had taken on its secondary role. It was now a gigantic spacecraft. It resembled the enigmatic flying saucers seen in the old days. What had previously been the domed roof of the building was now a viewing area from which the blackness of space was the dominant feature. The blue-green Earth was becoming smaller. Very few stars were visible in the firmament. They had long ago flown apart in the expanding Universe. The Milky Way was a shadow of its former self and the remnants of the whole galaxy were heading on a collision course with the neighbouring surviving stars of the Andromeda nebula.

The Space Ark carried its human cargo towards a distant and lonely astral speck of light. It would take several human generations before the craft would arrive at its destination. John, Sylvie and Jane remained in dormant survival mode within their stasis chambers hidden below the floor. The other humans by now had been released from their storage vats and were busy exploring their surroundings, forming social groups and pair bonding. The released children had quickly been integrated into family groups overseen by the adults. The knowledge downloaded into the brains by the implant devices ensured the humans knew how to obtain their nourishment and hydration. The craft quickly became home and a familiar place. The people did not recall their previous lives on the old Earth. In fact, they were unaware of the concept of planet Earth. The ship was their home. Those that peered out of the viewing dome could make out a distant pin prick of reflected light receding into the distance. This was not given much thought and little significance was attached to it.

The escape from the Earth was underway without any regrets or understanding by its human sons and daughters.

CHAPTER 8

A Galactic Journey

The Space Ark continued on its pre-set course. The shielding system did its job. The inhabitants of the vehicle were completely unaware that they were being protected from external harmful emissions. Cosmic rays and particles bombarded the ship but were either absorbed or deflected. Had this not been the case, the travellers would have suffered badly or even died as a result of radiation sickness and detrimental genetic mutations. While John, Sylvie and Jane mindlessly passed time in their storage vats, the remaining population within the ship thrived. The people released from the storage vats had received implants which downloaded into their brains everything they needed to know about survival on the ship. The ship was their world. It was a familiar place where life continued. It would have been hard for them to grasp the concept that they existed inside a large 'flying box' moving at near the speed of light. It was probably better for their social cohesion not to know the truth. It was a situation reminiscent of the distant past where not only the public but also government ministers and even presidents, prime ministers and heads of state were uninformed about the nature of UFOs as they had no 'need to know'.

The people released from storage in the stasis vats formed the first generation of space travellers. There were no social outcasts. They formed into small units and each group made certain areas of the craft their special 'homebase' or living area. In the first instance the implant programming had stimulated each adult male to seek an adult female mate and *vice versa*. This had gone very well. Couples paired off and quickly bonded. The pairing process was unrelated to racial type or physical attraction. It was an automated process initiated by stimulation of cerebral pathways by the neural implants. For the people in the Space Ark, there was no concept of country of origin. There was no knowledge or memory of the existence of the Americas', Europe, Africa, Asia or Australasia. Any remembrance of past family lives on the old Earth had been erased. They were people without any history.

Fortunately, as things worked out, men and women paired off without anyone being left out as a 'single' person. The programming system of the implants had taken into account the possibility that following the pairing process, there might be a male or a female left without a partner. In this instance the programming would have encouraged the formation of an adult unit in the form of a threesome, either two men and one woman or two women and one man. In the event, this situation did not arise. As time passed by, the paired adults developed feelings of affection for their partner and a desire to co-operate with other male and female paired units.

Children had been released from the storage vats some while after the adults. This had given the adults a chance to find a partner. Following their release, they wandered in a somewhat insecure frame of mind around the ship. When they approached the vicinity of paired adults, the brain implant devices triggered powerful maternal and paternal protective instincts. These ensured that the child would be welcomed as an addition to the unit. Bonding soon occurred and the units formed were akin to family units though there was no genetic link binding the individuals together as relatives. Where very small children or babies were encountered, the females would accept them for nurturing and they were placed in their care.

The fabric of the new society aboard the ship consisted of paired adult units and their associated child 'add-ons'. This first generation had no hierarchy. There was no conflict and co-operation, goodwill and friendship were normal. Some individuals were programmed with special attributes such as medical knowledge and skills and these were put to effective use. Any adjustments or repairs to technological devices were taken care of by automated failsafe systems. The people were able to continue making ongoing use of food and drink applicators and waste disposal systems without any major malfunctions occurring.

Systems were in place to dispose of bodies in the event of a death. Again, the knowledge of what to do was programmed into the minds of the people. Anyone who died would have their body placed into a cupboard-like enclosure in the wall of the ship. Sliding the door sealed off the body from the ship so it could no longer be seen by the people inside. The 'cupboard' was in fact an air-seal. After sliding the door, the space inside the cupboard 'disposal unit' was no longer air-tight. After a short delay, an opening appeared in the outer wall of the craft and the body was ejected into outer space. The process was rather like a burial at sea. When the internal door slid back to the open position, the body had vanished.

The community aboard the ship gradually developed more complex social groups and relationships. The implant technology allowed the people to have a degree of independent thought and action. Procreation occurred and the women gradually fell pregnant and delivered children who would become part of the next generation on the ship. The children 'adopted' by the adult pairs matured and soon the onboard population grew. After individuals became sexually mature they found partners, mated and produced their own progeny.

The genetic diversity among the occupants of the craft was expansive and this would have pleased John had he been aware of it. John continued along with his wife and daughter-in-law to pass months in stasis while the human society on the ship evolved. Months slowly turned into years.

Life on the Space Ark developed a form of daily routine. There was a twenty four hour cycle of the internal illumination system within the craft. Although there was no such experience as night and day, regular periods of dimming allowed the human bodies to develop circadian rhythms and regulate activities based on a 'body clock'. This enabled periods of sleep to alternate with more active periods. There were no schools, no libraries, no cinemas nor any forms of entertainment or leisure. The potential for boredom was real but the implant programming did encourage communal get-togethers in which the children of the first generation of space travellers were fully involved. The knowledge and skills provided to the individuals released from the storage vats by the neural implants were passed down to the next generation by word of mouth. Succeeding generations lived their lives without the interference of implant technology. New generations of humans continued to replace the old.

Information passed from generation to generation. Each generation taught the following one the skills and knowledge passed down by the preceding one. The generational information flow was akin to story-telling. The generational knowledge and traditions passing onwards began to take on a 'myth-like' quality. Stories, both real and imagined, began to circulate about ancestors. When mortal bodies reached the point of demise they were removed from the ship via the disposal units. Departure rituals developed resembling religious prayers to say goodbye to the dead. The days of simply depositing dead bodies in the disposal units and removing them were gone. Debate raged as to where the disposed bodies had gone. A view arose that they were taken to another place where they lived again. Their fate depended on their popularity. It was suggested that some would go into the 'great darkness' (outer space) and be swallowed up while others would enter the 'light beacons' (stars) and live again. These ideas were influenced by what could be seen from the viewing area in the dome. From here, the vast blackness of space was visible along with the occasional twinkle of one of the few remaining distant stars. The concept of hell and heaven was reborn.

The origin of the environment in which the unsuspecting occupants lived came under debate. Some believed that their living area had always existed and would continue to exist forever. An outrageous suggestion was put forward suggesting that the living environment had not always existed. It was formed suddenly out of nothing and one day it would come to an end. These two views were incompatible. At first the new suggestion was merely ridiculed. The revolutionary new idea was then expanded upon. It was suggested that not only did the living environment as known have a finite beginning and end, there were probably more living environments. There could be many of them. The arguments raged and had an uncanny resemblance to current ideas of the possible existence of a multiverse and multidimensions. The people aligned themselves within one or other of the two groups. Arguments and debates over the truth became fierce.

Society within the craft began to split into two camps. This situation was confined to the level of debate to start with but as new generations were born on the craft, people sided with one 'tradition' or the other. On one hand there were the 'believers' who felt that things had always been as they were and had never changed and never would. On the other hand there were the 'non-believers' who were sure there had been some kind of beginning and there would be an ending at some time in the future. Within each group were individuals with scientific knowledge passed down by predecessors including aspects of the nomenclature of fundamental particles and subatomic structures. The two groups used this background knowledge to identify themselves as believers or non-believers. The former became known as Muons and the latter as Pions.

Tensions built up between the Muons and Pions. With the passage of time, the two groups formed separate communities which mingled less and less. The Muons mainly grouped together on the wide ramps accessing different floors, corridors and small rooms of what was once the spherical building. Muons sometimes entered the area which had held the storage vats including the section where John, Sylvie and Jane continued in stasis hidden below surface level. The Pions occupied the more spacious areas of the expansive storage rooms and medical theatre sections and so had better facilities nearer to hand. The Muons gradually began to despise the Pions and only interacted with them at the border of the two communities which occupied different areas of the ship. The Pions tolerated the Muons but felt them to be non-imaginative and set in their thoughts.

The pairing of young Muons and Pions became frowned upon but from time to time a male and female from each group pair-bonded. This became a significant issue and the couple would have to choose between separating or living in either a Muon or Pion area. The production of children from such opposed astral faith pairings was discouraged by both groups.

There had never been a need for law enforcement or a military presence within the Space Ark. The founders had not even considered the need for such agencies. It was believed that no crime was likely to occur. What was there to steal? All needs were catered for. The first generation of released people had no memory of historical wars or rivalries, crimes or racial discrimination. Surely the onboard community would develop in a harmonious way? However, the relationship between the Muons and Pions continued to deteriorate. Some individuals within each group spoke badly of the other. The seeds of hatred and distrust had germinated. There was no intermediary available to step in and maintain order between the two groups.

The differences between Muons and Pons continued to widen. They developed differing traditions as ongoing generations were born, died and gave way to the next. The two groups became readily identifiable. The Muons took to wearing red wristbands while the Pions wore blue ones. The prayer-like words on eliminating the dead became fixed and repeatable but those spoken to the departing dead body were different depending on whether it was Muon or Pion. Muons did not attend dead body expulsion ceremonies of the Pions and *vice versa*. Even the food choices took on differences. Despite the fact that food replicator technology generated a variety of foods, the flavours and tastes favoured by the Muons came to differ from those of Pions.

The cultural separation between Muons and Pions continued to increase. Tolerance between the groups became lower and lower. Generational divides made the situation worse and views and attitudes became entrenched. For the first time, violent confrontations occurred accompanying the arguments between the communities. It took very little to ignite a problem. The two groups continued their mutual journey through space towards an unknown destination. They travelled together within their own mutual 'bubble' blowing across the vastness of outer space. An alien observer might have considered the onboard behaviour to be primitive and pathetic when seen in the perspective of the bigger picture of the long space voyage and quest for survival. There was no bigger picture to the Muons and Pions. Daily life continued within the ship and all everyday needs were catered for by the inbuilt technology.

On one fateful occasion a dispute arose between a Muon and a Pion. They had started a reasonably amicable discussion on the topic of the origin of the environment (within the Space Ark). The discussion between the believer and non-believer became more heated and more personal. After a period of argumentation, the Pion laughed at the Muon and suggested that his beliefs "bordered on the insane and were most improbable." The Pion continued his attack by saying "Muons do not use the logical part of their brains, their outlook was based on faith alone and fantasy." There was no immediate response from the Muon. He stood eye to eye with his protagonist. "Blasphemy is not acceptable" said the Muon under his breath. He reached out and grabbed a nearby laser device used in surgical procedures. He turned it on. The beam was directed directly towards the eyes of the Pion at close range. The device was set at full power and it burnt a hole through one eye, blinding him. The intense beam then penetrated deep into the delicate brain tissue behind the eyeball and destroyed the cells. The Pion man dropped dead on the spot. The Muon was far from shocked or sorry for what he had done. On the contrary, he was proud to have eliminated the non-believer. Perhaps this would be the first of many such eliminations. He 'whooped' with delight but then felt it prudent to quickly return deep into his own area of the ship as the Pions would not be pleased and soon they would be seeking retribution.

In due course the body was discovered and the cadaver was removed via the disposal unit with much pomp and praise. He was a martyr to the cause of Pion non-belief. The Pion community endeavoured to stay calm and sent a delegation to the Muons to soothe things down and try to find out who had done such a bad thing. Even if the perpetrator was to be handed over to them, the Pions did not know what to do with him. There was no criminal justice system. Could they punish him?

What would be the punishment? Was execution appropriate? There were no facilities for incarceration. Anyway, what if the person that did the deed was mentally ill? Should he be given treatment? There was a fear that such foul deeds might escalate and become commonplace. A number of Pions did not favour the conciliatory route and demanded retaliatory action. There was an urgent need to do 'something'.

A small Pion delegation was organised and met with their counterparts from the Muon community. The Pions had decided upon a policy of appeasement. They would appeal to the goodwill of the Muons to ensure that no further unfortunate deaths occurred. In the interests of peace they would not ask for the person who undertook the homicide to be handed over. The meeting resembled that of a much earlier time when in the 1930s following a meeting with Hitler, Chamberlain waved a piece of paper saying "peace in our time." The discussions between Pions and Muons were completed in a sea of smiles and reassurances. The Pion delegation returned to its community stronghold and boasted of success. The meeting concluded that what had happened was unfortunate but it was a one-off event. Two days later, a Muon couple were found dead in an area associated more commonly with Pion presence. They both had received fatal blows to the head. Clearly believers could no longer mix safely with non-believers and *vice versa*.

The Muon and Pion communities were now at complete loggerheads. In fact, the situation was even grimmer than might have been supposed. There was a strong outcry for revenge from militants of both communities. The Pions occupied most of the primary locations on the ship. There was a call to deny the Muons access to the medical areas. Some wanted to cut the Muons off from the food and water outlets. Others suggested a raid into the Muon areas of the ship with a warlike violent attack.

Eventually, an attitude of restraint prevailed. The Pions felt they had to protect themselves from the Muons and this was their main objective. The first thing to do was undertake separation. Barriers needed to be put in place to separate the two communities. These would be positioned to restrict Muon movement and keep them out of Pion territory. They would be allowed limited access to the medical facilities but any Muon encroaching into Pion areas would be supervised. The Muons had their own sources of food and drink but these were limited compared to those available to Pions. The Pions felt it would also be a good thing for the Muons not to have access to the life support systems which were under Pion control.

The issues between Muons and Pions continued over the next couple of generations and the young people in particular were raised in a situation where they had no experience of the previous harmonious existence on board the Space Ark in the not too distant historical times. The co-operation and friendships of the generation of individuals released from the stasis vats had long faded into history. There were in fact no memories of a time when there was just one community on the ship. People assumed there had always been Muons and Pions and they were destined to despise each other. Coexistence was almost intolerable.

The Pion community contained most of the onboard scientists, 'medics' and engineers. They considered themselves to be the enlightened group. Pions considered Muons to be backward-thinking and aggressive. Muons did not have any capacity for innovation or for novel ideas. They felt the Muons should be left to their own devices and kept away from the superior Pion people. The Muons posed a threat both physically and as a disruptive influence to the Pion views of non-belief.

The Muons considered that they were treated by Pions as a 'second class' community. The Pions were pompous and condescending. The Muons felt that the environment would be a better place if everyone accepted their version of the truth where the world as they knew it within the ship had always existed and would continue to do so. Society would be better off without Pions and their ideas. Any way of increasing the death rate of Pions was a good way. Perhaps a surprise militaristic mass raid on the Pions would result in their extermination. After all, they were non-believers.

It was during this period of social unrest and tension that both communities observed that one of the pinprick beacons of light seen in the great blackness was becoming brighter and larger. The Muons took this to be an indication that the Pions were developing some kind of exotic weapon to use against them. The Pions were not sure what to make of the observation but supposed that some technological malfunction might be occurring.

CHAPTER 9

Arrival

The Space Ark had travelled a long way through space and time since it left the futuristic planet Earth with its sun intent upon flooding its solar companion with deadly emanations. The journey time could be measured in light years. Generation after generation of human cargo reproduced, died and gave rise to another generation. This cycle was ongoing and allowed human existence to survive and continue. The designers of the Space Ark had done a wonderful job. The advanced technology had sustained the human occupants of the ship throughout its long voyage.

There had been many changes in the human population over time. The occupants had long since forgotten about the Earth and the ship was the only home they had known. They did not know they were travelling through space in a craft moving at high velocity. The ship was their Earth. In fact, the ship was their known Universe. Perhaps it was surprising that communal life on the ship had remained peaceful for so long. Problems only began with the advent of astral religions.

Life tended to follow ongoing cycles of existence. The people initially had remained in a cohesive group in which individuals helped each other and co-operation was the accepted mode of life. Many aspects of life were Utopian as there was little or no greed, crime or conflicts. A few cases of jealousy occurred from time to time where one member of a mated pair desired the body of someone from another pairing. Society had solved this issue in different ways over the years. Usually self-control was the solution but sometimes a male or female of one pair would share their sexual services with another.

The relatively recent social evolution of Muon and Pion 'faiths' represented a major change in the social history of the people in the Space Ark. The appearance of two astral religions had served to split the community into two factions. Each faction knew that their views were right. Also, each faction preferred that the other should convert to their beliefs or ideas but if this was not possible then the two groups needed to stay separate from each other. The situation deteriorated to the extent that the two groups reached the point of violent confrontation.

A large sphere could be seen clearly from the viewing area in the roof of the ship. It was visible to both Muons and Pions. The sphere became larger and larger until it was gigantic and began to block out the great blackness. The Space Ark was finally arriving at its programmed destination. It was now coming very near to a new Earth-like planet with continents showing green plant life and blue watery seas. Instruments around the ship became active for the first time in many years and warning lights began to flash. Audible proclamations announced that they were arriving at their new home called Terra Nova. Both the Muon and Pion communities were filled with fear. The Muons accused the Pions of producing a psychological weapon to terrify their community. The Pions felt that the time had come for their known Universe to be destroyed and it was 'the end of days' as had been predicted in their views about creation and destruction. In many respects they were correct.

John's stasis vat started to rise from below floor level and the emerald green contents of the sustaining fluid drained away.

Moments later the vats containing Sylvie and Jane also rose from their hidden site below the floor and the pink medium slithered away through outlet filters. The vats continued to rise and it was not long before the three people were released from stasis. John's mind was quick to clear. He realised that he and his two family companions had been stored away for many years. He quickly regained his memories including his failed attempt to repopulate the Earth and the disastrous experiment in which many of his subjects had perished due to deadly solar exposure. He knew that since he had now been released, the ship must be approaching the new planet which would become home to the ship's occupants. Standing next to him were his wife Sylvie and his daughter-in-law Jane. The minds of Sylvie and Jane took longer to clear than his. As their memories were gradually regained, some of the thoughts in their minds became unsettling but John was quick to step into reassuring mode and he quickly calmed the two women.

Sylvie remembered how she had met John and married 'a man from the future'. She had loved him and bore him a son. John had returned to the future leaving her to care for their son Kevin. She had never discussed her husband with other people nor told anyone about what she had learned about the problems of the future Earth. Sylvie had enjoyed her life raising her son Kevin and recalled how he had supported her at a time when thyroid surgery resulted in the extraction of an implant device from her neck which she now knew had influenced her decisions, behaviours and memories. Sylvie recalled with pleasure the marriage of son Kevin to Jane and how she had befriended Jane's mum, Emma. Sylvie had also become very close to Jane and she became more like a daughter than a daughter-in-law. They had spent a lot of time together.

John quickly described to Sylvie the final events of her life on the old Earth. She was aged in her sixties and had taken a walk through the local woods. During this stroll she passed through a time portal into the future and made her way into the spherical building. She had been maintained in a safe storage state for many years and the stasis fluid had not only sustained her but helped upgrade a physiological rejuvenation process which occurred during her passage through the time portal. This had enabled her to regain much of her physical youthfulness and looks.

Jane's recovery from stasis took the longest and she remained disoriented and confused for some time. She recognised Sylvie and this had a calming influence even though she could not understand why she looked younger than how she remembered her. Some of Jane's final conscious memories were tinged with trauma but she also recalled good times. Sylvie gave Jane a reassuring hug and this reinforced the bonding that had formed between the two women many years ago. John surprised himself and gave a hug not only to Sylvie but also to his daughter-in-law Jane for the first time.

Jane's memories suddenly began to flood back and the gaps were filled by explanations from both John and Sylvie. Jane clearly remembered her youthful flirtation with Kevin, John and Sylvie's son, in the woodland near her home. She remembered how deeply her emotions ran when she fell in love with Kevin. Her wedding day had been wonderful and marriage to Kevin stood out as a very significant and happy period of her life. She had been very pleased when they moved into their own house. She smiled at the memories of her career as a midwife. She had undertaken satisfying employment and done a good job. She had interacted very professionally with her patients. Jane also recalled with pride Kevin's career in genetic research.

The memory recall process was not all a positive experience for Jane as bad events were recovered by her mind as well as good ones. One terrible event brought tears to Jane's eyes when she remembered hearing the news that her mum Emma had passed away on a trip to Australia.

Other memories returned to Jane randomly and not all of them were about major life events. Jane recalled a nice evening at an Indian restaurant in the local village and a great spicy meal served in person by the manager called Mohinder, long since passed away and turned to dust. Oh yes, she then recalled the time she had to have surgery on her neck area. A strange object had been removed from a spinal disc which turned out to be similar to the one removed from Sylvie's thyroid gland. The nature of the implant was quickly explained to Jane by her father-in-law John but she was unsure that she approved of its functions of mind control, body monitoring, communication and information downloading. The mind control aspect in particular seemed to be a morally outrageous function and a clear assault on personal liberty. It was apparent to Jane that the latter concept was alien to John.

Jane's mind then regained the most traumatic part of her past life memories and they made her shudder. She did not feel anger but was overwhelmed with anguish and maternal concern. Jane remembered that she had become pregnant. Her labour had started and she had got into the car with Kevin in order to give birth in the relatively safe environment of a nearby hospital maternity unit. Kevin had taken another route and they had ended up in the woods where Kevin had made her walk along a woodland pathway. What happened after that was still rather hazy. John explained that she had passed through a time portal device into the future and entered the spherical building. More of the memories of what happened then came back to Jane. She had entered some kind of medical theatre and lay on a strange floating table. Kevin had delivered their baby. He was acting very strangely and Jane had wondered if he had lost his mind. She had begged him to give her their baby. Kevin referred to their baby as Amy.

John explained to Jane that she had been placed in a storage vat which nurtured her and kept her in good health in a suspended state of stasis for a long time period. Both she and Sylvie had just been released from storage to resume their lives. John explained that he himself had been in stasis and had also just been released. Jane interrupted John and asked him where her baby was and if she was alive. She also wanted to know what had happened to Kevin.

John continued with his explanation. Kevin had placed an implant device in baby Amy's neck. This had been necessary because she was to play an important part in an experiment to save the whole of humankind. Kevin had returned to the old Earth at a time just a few years after Jane's departure into the future. Jane need not have any concerns. Amy had been returned to the old Earth when she was eight and was under the care of her father. Her memories were programmed by the implant to begin at age eight. Kevin had been a great single parent and had cherished their daughter as she developed towards adulthood. At this point in the explanations Jane felt robbed of the maternal experience of raising her child. She began to feel ambivalent emotions towards her father-in-law John. However, there was nothing she could do about what had happened and she continued to listen intently to the rest of the explanation.

John outlined what had happened in the future Earth. Huge climatic and environmental changes had occurred as the sun aged and began to emit harmful radiation. The animals and plants on the Earth began to die and species after species became extinct. The human population also suffered badly. The scientists utilised their great technological knowledge to stave off human extinction. As the emissions from the sun intensified, the mortality rate soared. A Great Plan for survival had been produced. Using techniques of gene manipulation and gene therapy, it was hoped to introduce sufficient genetic diversity into the human population so that some individuals could withstand the ravages of the solar emissions and continue human existence on the future Earth. In order to accomplish this, John had used time portal technology to travel into past times so he could abduct potentially useful human stock and bring them into the future for breeding purposes. That is how John met his wife Sylvie. He had come across her in the distant past. He had unexpectedly fallen in love with her. They married and had their son Kevin. Although an implant was placed in Sylvie's neck she was a willing participant and wanted to help John in his endeavours to repopulate the future Earth.

John explained that he had intended to bring Jane's daughter Amy back into the future after she had been parented by Kevin and reached sexual maturity. His granddaughter was genetically engineered such that her gene constitution might contribute positively towards survival on the future Earth. John did not expect that his son Kevin would argue with him about doing such a thing. After all, Kevin should have been under the influences of his implant. Despite this, Kevin wanted his daughter Amy to remain in her own time with him and be allowed to live a fulfilled lifespan in her own time zone. Eventually John had relented and allowed Amy to stay. On hearing this Jane felt very proud of Kevin and the stand he had made against his father's plans.

The explanation continued and came more up to date. John explained that the Great Plan ultimately had failed. Harmful solar radiation killed off his colleagues and the remnants of mankind. Life on the Earth had virtually disappeared except for a synthetic lifeform resembling blue-green grass that coated the ground. It had befallen John to be the saviour of the human race. The large spherical building on the future Earth was shielded against the harmful emissions of the sun but these defences could not be relied on to last forever.

Although John explained how intense harmful solar radiation had killed the people on Earth, he omitted the part about his decision to experiment on a large group and purposely expose them to the harmful solar emissions. The fact that five thousand people died because of his actions was one snippet of information he thought it wise to skirt round. John did not need to tell Sylvie and Jane 'additional irrelevant facts'. The external conditions had simply been too severe to support life. All that was left to do was to abandon mother Earth. Fortunately this scenario had been envisaged by John's scientist and engineer peers of his future time.

Leaving the Earth was only to be done as a final resort. The journey in the spherical building's secondary role as a fully automated spacecraft programmed to finding another Earth-like planet had lasted for many generations while John, Sylvie and Jane had been hidden away in stasis. Since all three of them were now free of stasis, arrival at the new Earth was imminent. It would not be too long before the ship went into automated landing mode and would set down on the surface of the planet.

Before entering stasis himself, John had set in motion the release programme of the small group of people from his 'prime group' of individuals sealed in storage vats near those of Sylvie and Jane. John had entered his own stasis vat and along with those of Sylvie and Jane had caused them to descend below floor level out of sight. This was achieved just prior to the release of the individuals of the prime group for safety reasons. After all, who knew what damage might be done to his vat or those of Sylvie and Jane by humans when they were set free or during the long voyage of the Space Ark. John felt that on balance it was more prudent to allow the small group of humans being released from the vats to breed and continue autonomous lives rather than keep them all in stasis for the duration of the long trip. Should something go wrong with the release mechanism from the vats, rather than keep the humans in stasis for perpetuity, at least some of the offspring via multi-generational reproduction would survive until the arrival at Terra Nova.

John looked in all directions and listened intently. Where were the people on the ship? Was John alone with Sylvie and Jane?

Sylvie and Jane had listened to John's lengthy discourse. There was little response from Sylvie. She seemed very accepting of everything John had said. She was pleased to see her husband again. Sylvie felt he was a great man and had battled so hard mainly by himself to save mankind. It crossed her mind that she would like to be reunited with her son Kevin and see her granddaughter Amy but for the moment her mind was transfixed on her incredible husband and she took his hand in hers. Jane on the other hand was less than impressed. It was rather hard to believe everything she had heard. John was the root cause of her being taken away from her husband and had caused her child to be removed from her care. This was monstrous. She tried to understand his actions in the context of attempting to save mankind as a whole.

John had not noticed any humans since he, Sylvie and Jane had been released from stasis. For a moment he feared that something had gone wrong and no humans had survived the multi-generational voyage on the Space Ark. He had neither seen nor heard anybody. John then heard some shuffling sounds which he put down to human presence and these became louder as they approached the room containing the three escapees from the stasis vats. At first John experienced joy as two Muons entered the room with their distinctive red wristbands. One was male and the other female. John's glee soon turned to dismay.

CHAPTER 10

A Primitive People

"Who are you?" asked the male Muon.

"I am a passenger like you and these two ladies are my companions" said John.

"I do not know what you are talking about" said the Muon. "Are you red or blue?"

"You will have to tell me what you mean" said John. "We have been 'asleep' for a long time. There are many things I need to both explain to you and ask you."

"Why do you bear no colour on your wrists? You have no band at all."

"I do not know of the need for a band" said John. "I do not know why colour is relevant."

"Have you been sent here by the Pions to cause confusion?" asked the Muon male.

"I do not know who or what a Pion is. Perhaps it is something that developed on this ship while we slept for such a long time" said John.

The female Muon spoke for the first time. "Blasphemy" she screamed. "You are Pion spies. You must be put to death."

The two Muons beckoned to John, Sylvie and Jane to move out of the room and move onwards along the connecting corridor. The two Muons followed them. As they passed along the corridor John quietly confided to Sylvie and Jane that they were about to pass a camouflaged entrance to a sealed off room and they had to find a way of distracting their two captors so they could gain entrance. When they reached the appropriate position in the corridor John spoke to the two Muons.

"Would you allow me to remain here alone with my two companions for a few minutes? We have awoken from a long sleep. There are a few issues we need to clarify in our heads in order to co-operate with you. We have not recovered properly from our period of rest. We will follow you in due course." John hoped to buy a little time to get the hidden hatchway unsealed. He did not like the way the humans on the ship had apparently evolved an aggressive and intolerant attitude. Having survived years of stasis, John had no intention of being put to death by some foolish misguided human descendant of the generation he had captured and abducted years before.

The female Muon raised a device located and attached to the top part of her hand and pointed it at John and his companions. It was clearly some kind of weapon. "Move" said the female Muon. "If you do not continue I will disintegrate you here and now and pass your remnants to your Pion friends to grieve over." Understandably, John continued to move along the corridor with Sylvie and Jane following on close behind. The two women were becoming fearful but John displayed and felt little emotion. His mind was concentrated on finding a way of getting himself and the two women into the hidden room.

The corridor opened into a room in which there was a large 'hotch-potch' of male and female Muons including children and babies. The group was truly multi-racial and genetically diverse. The group's behaviour and outlook surprised John in certain respects. They reminded him of primitive savage peoples he had experienced during his time jumps into the past to collect human specimens for his genetic experiments. All the people present wore red wristbands including the children and babies.

Their male Muon captor greeted the group and proclaimed a great discovery. "We have captured Pion spies. They bear no bands upon their wrists. They are confusers. They talked of being travellers and a ship. They blasphemed."

The female Muon captor made her own contribution to the announcement of the capture of John, Sylvie and Jane. "They must die. We brought them here for you to question before extermination. The females have not spoken. Only the male has spoken to us and misleads with talk about a long sleep."

A rather senior looking male with a grey beard and wispy hair stepped forward from the Muon group and came into close proximity to John and the two women. He stood before them and looked them up and down. It appeared that this man had some rank and influence. The Muon group watched in silence as he addressed the three new arrivals.

"Where have you been located? Why did the Pions send you? Why is there no coloured band on your wrists?"

Jane suddenly erupted in a fearful verbal response though John would have preferred her to remain silent. "We do not know what you are talking about. We don't know anything about wrist bands. We have no idea who Pions are. Leave us alone."

The Muon man came face to face with Jane and stared at her eyeball to eyeball like boxers of old at a press conference before a bout.

"You look Pion to me. Tell me the truth. Are you a non-believer?"

"Non-believer in what?" asked Jane.

The senior Muon male stepped backwards and considered his response. It was soon forthcoming. "The three of you do not belong with us Muons. Whether you are Pions or not is of no great importance. You are clearly non-believers. Your presence among our great Muon community must not be allowed to cause unrest. I do not know about any long sleep you mentioned to my fellow Muons who brought you here. I do not want to know. You will in due course be shown to the Pions so they know we have captured you and then you will be terminated and removed from the environment via a disposal unit. Whoever you are, your deaths will be a great warning to the Pions to stay away from us."

While the events with his captors had been unfolding, John had spied the approaching Terra Nova filling the viewing area. The planet was getting closer and closer. It would not be too long before the automated systems on the ship went into landing mode. They had been programmed long ago but still functioned perfectly. It was apparent to John that these Muons knew nothing about the voyage to a new Earth. They had no comprehension of what was being seen outside the ship. The ship was set to deliver a warning to its occupants regarding landing on the new planet and a brief historical evaluation of life on Earth and its evacuation due to its deadly sun. These Muons clearly would not cope with the news. They would not even believe what was in front of their own eyes.

The situation was similar to how things had once been on the old Earth. In the old days, flying saucers and other UFOs had been frequently captured on films, video cameras and camcorders. Strange beings had also been seen by many people during sessions of contact or abduction. The world at that time was in denial. Debunkers explained away the sightings and mocked the contactees and abductees. The sightings were due to Venus, weather balloons, flocks of birds, meteors, mistaken aircraft, secret military craft and so on. People having strange contact experiences with odd entities were deluded or were mentally ill. Even pilots seeing strange craft up close were mistaken. Humans would hold onto long held beliefs regardless of logic. Sometimes one hundred percent of people believed that something was the case. If the belief was factually wrong, it did not become true just because everybody believed it to be the case. This was a hard concept for humans to grasp, especially for those who held entrenched religious views. Humans believed things because they wanted to not because they were correct or factual.

"I can explain to you the view you see before you. I can tell you what it is. Do not harm us" said John. John pointed to the new planet Terra Nova in full sight through the viewing area. It was clearly visible for all to see.

The senior Muon man replied. "We know what it is. It is a Pion illusion. It is a trick designed to scare us. We know our environment is constant and never changing. The Pions are trying to make us have doubts. They are hateful. Their beliefs are anathema to us."

John's mind was sharp. He quickly picked up on the idea that the Pions must be other people on the ship that held a different view to the Muon captors. Evidently the groups were at loggerheads with each other, probably worse. "You are mistaken" said John.

"You are a liar and already seek to sow seeds of discontent. It will be good for all three of you to die."

Sylvie decided it was time to add her input to the exchange. She was quietly spoken but this was the time for an intervention. "No! This man is my husband. He does not lie. You may kill us but you will make a bad mistake and bring disaster down upon not only all Muons but all Pions too. There will be nobody alive at all. All I ask is that you listen to what my husband wishes to tell you. If you do not agree with what you hear then we cannot prevent you from eliminating us." Jane was surprised at Sylvie's confident and outspoken outburst. The two women were holding hands. Jane squeezed Sylvie's hand tightly.

The senior Muon man peered at Sylvie. He then cast his gaze towards John. "You may speak" he said.

John projected his thoughts in a very forceful manner. "I have a great revelation for you. There is something you must do before I can tell you. You must take me with my two companions to a safe place where we can meet with representatives of the Pions."

"We keep our distance from the non-believers. We do not want to be contaminated by their ideas. They keep away in their own places. They maintain many key areas and facilities for the benefit of Pions while Muons struggle. Pion intruders into Muon areas are not tolerated. They are eliminated."

"What happens to Muons who pass into Pion areas?" asked John.

"In the past the Pions absorbed them and brainwashed them to follow their own beliefs. We do not accept back anyone who enters the Pion areas. Anyone passing across the boundary between groups does so knowing they cannot return to us Muons. They are lost to the Pions forever. Should any of us cross the boundary by accident or be captured we encourage such Muon people to terminate themselves and take a Pion with them."

"You must take me with my two companions to the boundary area you talk of. It must be a safe place. Muons and Pions must be present. Can you arrange this? I ask you to trust me. I have news of something which will affect everything you know."

"I do not trust you" said the senior Muon man. "However, I trust the female who claimed you were her husband. She seemed sincere. It is possible to arrange such a meeting. A meeting will be arranged with Pions at a safe boundary between us. If you are wasting our time or engage support from the non-believers all three of you will immediately be eliminated."

John, Sylvie and Jane were kept within the Muon group and watched over. Time passed which seemed like hours but in due course the senior Muon male instructed them to follow him. They took a route through various corridors and rooms which were familiar to John from times long ago when the Space Ark served as a spherical building for his genetic engineering and breeding experiments. Accompanying them were the two Muons who had captured them in the room from where they had emerged from stasis. John noted that the female still carried the weapon and he was sure that she would have no hesitation using it at a moment's notice. He felt that not only would she use it on him, Sylvie and Jane but it would not need much provocation for her to blast the Pions they were about to meet.

The group entered a moderately sized room. There were three ways in or out. John, Sylvie and Jane entered the room through the inward corridor. There was another entrance corridor opposite from where they stood. John knew this led to a completely separate section of what was now a spaceship but formerly a large research facility in the spherical building. That was the area where the Pion community had based themselves. Over to the right was a narrow exit corridor. John knew that this followed a looping route but led back towards the area they had come from. It opened into the corridor not far from where the stasis vats had been situated. This was also close to the area where the hidden room was sealed away. The meeting location was a very good one and afforded John and his compatriots a possible route to reach the sealed off room.

The three Muons came to a standstill where the entrance corridor opened out into the room. They did not occupy the space in the middle of the room which was filled only by John and his two companions. Moments later three humans appeared at the opening of the corridor opposite from where the Muons stood. They also came to a standstill where their corridor entrance opened into the central space of the room and they did not enter the room itself. John observed that there were two females and one male. All three wore blue wristbands. These were Pion non-believers. It was not clear to John and his companions what it was that Pions did not believe but it did not matter. John and his partners stood at the centre of the room feeling exposed and vulnerable. They were in-between the Muon and Pion groups. There was silence. He needed to do some convincing or there would be a blood bath. He did not like the look of the Muon female with the weapon. She looked nervous and might show reckless destructive behaviour unless he did a good job. The Muons and Pions apparently did not wish to speak to each other. This was a very difficult situation.

It was clear that the Muons were filled with cynicism and had a low tolerance for anyone who did not wear the red wristband. They were suspicious of conspiracy between John and the despised Pions. The Pions for their part knew it was unusual to liaise with the primitive Muons so only something important would have caused them to arrange the meeting. They were suspicious of confrontation and deception and had no idea about what they were going to be told.

John addressed the onlookers. "I am going to tell you something you may not wish to hear. You must allow me to finish my statement because it affects both Muons and Pions equally. This place where you live is not all that exists. You are enclosed within a 'box' that is moving. You are within a huge machine. You know this place as your home. It has been the home of your ancestors for many years. There was a time when Muons and Pions were one group. Yes, you do not believe me but let me continue. There is an outside to this machine. Many years ago, this machine that contains you left an object called a planet. It was where you originated from. The planet could not sustain you. It was abandoned and this machine is a craft taking you to a new planet, a new beginning and a new home."

At this point the Muon female with the weapon interrupted the speech. "Just as I thought. You are talking nonsense. You spew Pion propaganda to confuse believers and disrupt our community. We know we exist within a Universe. This place is the Universe. It is all that there is and all that there has ever been. It will continue forever. It was a waste of time bringing you here. We should have terminated you earlier. You are fortunate that we are tolerant but you will not be permitted to haemorrhage Pion misinformation."

The Pion male had been listening intently and broke the silence from the Pion side of the room. "Wait! Muon, we do not know this man nor his two female compatriots. His story may be fantasy but he says both Pions and Muons are affected by the knowledge he claims to have. Let him continue."

There was an uneasy silence from the Muon party. The female with the weapon was vexed. She hated non-believers. Her hatred was all-encompassing. She had nothing but contempt for blue wristband wearers. Those with no wristband were equally guilty of blasphemy and disbelief. She raised her arm with the disruptor weapon in place with the intention of ending the proceedings once and for all. Her mind had made the decision that the strange people with no wristband must die. At the same time, she could eliminate the three Pion conspirators who stood opposite her as well. There would be little consequence or retribution. Pions tried to suppress violent thoughts and reprisals. They were weak. The Pions would send delegations with diplomatic agendas to the Muons when atrocities occurred. 'Peace in our time' was the goal of Pion appeasement.

"Let us hear the remnants of your message. Make it brief" said the male Muon. He took his female compatriot's arm and forcefully lowered it so the weapon pointed harmlessly downwards. Like his female comrade, he was not averse to ridding the area of the non-wristband wearers and the blue wristband wearers but knowledge of the full message might be useful information for the Muon community in their efforts to nullify any further disinformation originating from the hated Pions.

"I can prove my words are true" said John. "You only need observe over there." John pointed towards the globe of Terra Nova now filling the visual field observable from the viewing area. "That is your new home. This machine that encloses you is about to take you there. You will not be allowed to stay here. You will have to start a new existence whether you like it or not. Muons and Pions will have to co-operate and live as one unit. If you do not do this you will all die."

The Muons were enraged. The female Muon with the weapon looked as if she was about to suffer apoplexy. Even the Pions were not impressed. The idea of co-operating with Muons was far-fetched. The Muons were beneath contempt. They were primitive and violent and were best left to their own devices out of sight and preferably out of mind of the Pion community.

The female Muon raised her weapon. No-one was going to stop her this time. Sylvie and Jane hugged each other. This was the end. Even John felt that nothing more could be done. All his efforts to save mankind had finally come to this. He was going to be blasted out of existence. That was his reward for his diligent research to save mankind and translocate the surviving people of the prime group to a place of safety.

At that very moment the ship began shuddering violently. A humming noise began of such high frequency and intensity it felt as if the ear drums would burst under the cascade of vibrations. The walls of the great ship turned a bright yellow colour reminiscent of sunflowers in full bloom. Sounds oscillated back and forth. The floor of the ship became unsteady as the craft entered the atmosphere of Terra Nova and made automated changes in pitch, roll and yaw as it determined its final flight path and sought a landing zone to touch down in a safe area.

John knew it would be a shameful disaster for the Space Ark to have flown across interstellar space on a long voyage and successfully located its final destination only to crash and kill all the occupants at the last step. The 'end of days' proposed by Pions was a real possibility.

Computerised voices sang out warning messages and instructions. "Warning, warning, landing in progress. Warning, warning, landing in progress. Secure position, brace for impact. Secure position, brace for impact." The ship was programmed to deliver its human occupants as safely as possible. Instructions were broadcast in simple language loud enough for all on board to hear. It was up to the human cargo to respond appropriately.

The Muon and Pion delegations looked at each other with a mixture of fear and confusion. The female Muon was still considering blasting John but part of her mind was trying to understand what was happening around her and this distraction saved John's life.

"Go back to your communities" said John. "It is time for change. Muons and Pions must live together. Live and populate the new world." John beckoned to Sylvie and Jane to follow him. The threesome made a rapid exit through the side corridor and headed in the direction of the room where they had emerged from their storage vats. John did not want to remain in further contact with Muons or Pions. They were now fearful and confused. The female with the weapon might lose her constraint at any moment and wreak death with her device.

Muons and Pions all over the spacecraft were panicking and behaving erratically. They would be fortunate to survive the landing without taking casualties, some caused by their own actions. John hoped that the two communities would work together but he did not intend to be captured again by any of the ship's occupants. He needed to reach the sealed room in the corridor that had been hidden from view for so long.

The threesome reached the desired area without encountering any contact with others. Neither Muons nor Pions were in pursuit. The part of the wall of the corridor which interested John was barely distinguishable from the other parts. Sylvie and Jane were confident in John's instructions but hidden away in the recesses of their minds they hoped he knew what he was doing. John placed both hands flat against the corridor wall and pushed. It was as if he were trying to make an impression of his hands in a soft clay medium. Beneath their feet it was possible to feel the dropping motion of the ship as it descended. It was making a controlled landing but the Muons and Pions were undergoing a great trauma. It was time for John and his relatives to leave.

The wall changed hue as the atomic particles made a paradigm shift and it became possible to pass right through it into the small room beyond. John entered first, closely followed by Sylvie and Jane. The corridor wall returned to its normal configuration and texture, sealing off the entrance from the rest of the ship. There was very little space inside the room. It was somewhat like an 'under-the-stairs cupboard' found in many current houses and not much bigger. It was certainly cramped for three people and it was almost impossible to turn round. The space was more than claustrophobic. Sylvie and Jane were worried. They could not survive for long in that tiny enclosed space. The confining little room was very dimly illuminated and not a desirable place to spend ones time.

John, Sylvie and Jane could hear instructions being given to the people inhabiting the ship via broadcast sound systems. Information flowed regarding coping with the landing and subsequent exit procedures for escaping from the bowels of the craft. The Space Ark was in the last throes of its long life and duties. The Muons and Pions were being given instructions on survival and would be provided with sufficient items and technology for survival to get them off to a good start in their new world. Sylvie and Jane had no desire to be included in the landing party disembarking on Terra Nova. Neither did they wish to be marooned in the tiny space in the wall of the craft. All they could make out in the facing wall was a triangular area bounded by a dark line with its apex at just above head height and with its sides just wider than body width.

John applied his hands to the wall adjacent to the triangular shape. The boundary of the triangle began to glow and flash colours. The colours alternated in appearance...red, green, blue...red, green, blue. A soft hum filled the air. Many years ago both Sylvie and Jane had passed through a larger but similar device which had been situated in woodland near their village homes. They had passed into the device and emerged into the future Earth. The technology was sophisticated and the fruit of years of research by great scientists and engineers. It could catapult individuals through spacetime by warping the fabric of space. It was possible to programme the device and set emergence locations and times specifically tuned to the body parameters of individuals. Features such as pupil identification, voice recognition, fingerprints and DNA constituency allowed the device to be set to a particular destination for each individual person using the device.

John had been a frequent user enabling him to abduct humans from the distant past and bring them into the future with him for genetic and human breeding studies. The machine acted like a wormhole through which one could pass via temporal and spatial pathways. The portal was also transdimensional and teleportable in functionality.

"What is happening?" asked Sylvie.

"I am scared" said Jane.

"Follow me into this device" instructed John. "You are going home. You are going back to your time. Your memories will stay with you but some may have a dreamlike quality. Sylvie, we will be together again on your old Earth and this time we will have a life together."

"What will the effect be when we go back?" asked Sylvie. "If we go back to live in the past knowing what we now know, how will future history be affected?"

John looked at his wife. "I am a man of the future...but do you expect me to know the answer to everything?" he asked. He had a smile on his face. John looked unworried about life's problems for the first time in many years.

"What will become of me?" enquired Jane.

"You, my dear, will be reunited with your husband. There will have been a time gap since you two were together but Kevin will know who you are. I know my son still loves you. You will also get to meet your beautiful daughter Amy. It was me who caused you to be deprived of contact with your daughter since the time she was born and for that I am sorry. Try to forgive me. I did a little genetic tinkering with her to adapt her body to the future environment before she was returned to Kevin's care. I had planned that she would develop and mature before being returned to the future to help repopulate the Earth. As you know I decided that this was not the right thing for me to do. Kevin has Amy in his care. She will be fine and beautiful like you Jane, her lovely blonde blue eyed mother."

Jane relished the prospect of resuming life with Kevin and finally being able to spend time with her daughter would be a dream come true. Jane knew that Amy would no longer be a baby and that she had missed out on many years of Amy's development but nevertheless as far as contact with her daughter was concerned, it was better late than never. Jane's lips curled upwards in a broad smile. The prospect of forgiving John his actions was not on her current agenda.

There was no time for such considerations in the present circumstances.

"The ship is landing" said John. "Quickly! Follow me into the time portal. Do not be afraid." John stepped forward into the space bounded by the triangle of flashing lights and duly disappeared from sight.

"You go next" said Sylvie. "Trust John…he would not let you come to any harm."

Jane was scared. She wanted so much to return to the Earth she used to know and be with her husband and daughter. It was so hard for her to take in everything that had happened. Everything was becoming increasingly surreal. It would take a 'leap of faith' to plunge her body into this tiny space which was supposedly a time portal. She hesitated. Jane turned and looked at Sylvie. She was smiling. Jane knew it was time to go. She plunged head first into the triangular space as if she were at a swimming pool and plunging off the diving boards into the water below. Jane was gone.

The landing ship bounced and threw Sylvie to one side. The noise was deafening. Creaking and vibrating noises filled the air. There were a few distant screams and some shouting. Acrid smoke began to seep into the small room. The outside mechanical noises of the landing craft ceased.

The Space Ark had landed in a safe place. The landing itself had been heavy. Many of its systems were closing down. Exit doors had opened to allow the occupants to leave. Computerised messages on survival continued to blast out instructions to the human population. Muons and Pions would need to put their differences to one side if they were going to survive. Terra Nova may well have been a new home but it was not the Earth. Its degree of hostility or friendship to humans was yet to be discovered. It had a complex orbit round one sun of a binary star system. There were two moons visible overhead. One was about the same size and distance away as would have been familiar to someone on the old Earth. The other moon was huge and great craters on its surface were clearly visible with the naked eye. The sun rode high in the sky and was a healthy looking bright yellow disc. It was much more amenable to human existence than its far away ancient cousin who had turned blood red and spewed lethal radiation across the old Earth.

Sylvie was all alone. She had been slightly bruised during the landing of the ship. She hoped the people in the craft were all unharmed and would be able to make a life for themselves on the new planet. She did not wish the Muons and Pions any harm. It would be good to think that humanity could continue to survive albeit on a planet far distant from mother Earth.

Sylvie noticed that the brightness of the flashing lights adorning the boundary of the triangular opening was decreasing. The frequency at which the flashing was occurring was also declining. Sylvie suddenly feared that she might be trapped on this new planet with the ship's occupants. Perhaps she would be made to choose between becoming a Muon or a Pion. Even worse, maybe she might be trapped within the tiny room she now occupied alone and could die entombed in the tiny space.

Sylvie pushed her hand into the space beyond the triangular opening. She encountered resistance. It felt very much like pushing a hand hard against a thin rubbery sheet that bends with the pressure but does not break. It was akin to being trapped inside a giant rubber glove and trying to force your way out or being inside a large inflated balloon and attempting to push through the rubbery boundary to burst it and escape. Sylvie pushed her body against the entrance to the portal but could not enter. The boundary was some kind of 'event horizon' similar to that which surrounds a black hole in space. Once passing that point matter and energy were sucked in and could not return unless another portal device was situated at the destination site. Sylvie wanted to be sucked in but she could not force her way in. The boundary of the time portal was closing fast, separating the future from the past where she wished to return forever.

There was little space to gain momentum in the small room to take a run at the interface but Sylvie managed to take a couple of steps backwards. She then accelerated her body and raised her legs as she attempted to breach the barrier between the future and the past, feet first. She was rather like a high jump specialist raising her legs to leap over the bar. She would try a feet first approach combined with a leap off the ground to utilise her full body weight. There was a feeling like an elastic sheet stretching across the boundary of the portal. She had to break through it somehow. Sylvie's legs passed across the boundary into the vortex and she 'sank' into the void but only as far as her pelvis. Her upper torso, head and arms remained in the small room within the now landed ship while her lower body, legs and feet dangled in an unknown place in warping spacetime. She wriggled and struggled to insert the rest of her body. Sylvie was in a quicksand which was refusing to pull her below the surface. She kicked her legs for all she was worth and began to feel pain at the level of her pelvic bones as they became squeezed as the portal closed. Sylvie was scared that she might be chopped in half or that part of her body might transfer into the past leaving the other half to perish in the future.

Lactic acid was building up in Sylvie's leg muscles from her heavy kicking movements. She ceased kicking for a moment to rest her muscles as she was cramping. She regained just enough strength for one last effort. She did not know how long the opening of the time portal would remain viable but she was sure there was not long to go before it closed forever. Sylvie inhaled a huge breath and gasped as she gave an almighty kick with both legs. Her body slithered through the opening moments before it sealed itself. Her body entered a strange realm within a vortex. It was like she had given the final push when giving birth which expelled a baby. She had entered the spacetime vortex. Time and space became indistinguishable as Einstein's Laws were violated using concepts that he himself had envisaged. The warping of space allowed Sylvie to follow John and Jane through the closing wormhole to emerge safely on the other side.

CHAPTER 11

The Return: a New Earth

People spilled out of the landed craft. They did not have time to consider who was a Muon or who was a Pion. The ship had landed heavily and there was impact damage and a degree of smoke. The only topic of immediate consideration was escape. Other issues could wait, survival was the main concern. Mothers clutched their children as they scrambled out of the craft and onto the ground. The younger adults sought missing relatives and aided the older and less able occupants of the Space Ark to exit. There were even cases where Muons assisted Pions and *vice versa*. The scramble to get out of the ship intensified as metallic grating noises from the disassembling vehicle filled the air.

The exit from the craft was far from orderly and there was much panic and trepidation. The forced expulsion from the bowels of the ship was at best a cultural shock and at worst a catastrophe for all concerned. The Space Ark had been the all-encompassing Universe. There was no known 'outside' yet the present reality revealed that an external environment existed. The Muon belief that the ship was the known Universe and had always existed and would always continue was shattered. The cultural shockwave would run deep and leave many aghast. Some Muons would come to contemplate whether life was worth living with their cultural belief system blown away.

A UFO landing on the White House lawn would prove the existence of aliens but the cultural shock to society and destruction of ingrained belief systems might destabilise the current world. Many religious doctrines would be proved to be based on myths. Society could easily disintegrate into mayhem generating violence and rioting. The landing of their spacecraft home and subsequent expulsion represented a similar traumatic shock to the Muons. Even the Pions who held that the Universe (within the ship) had a beginning in a great creation event and one day would be destroyed in a calamitous reversal could barely cope with what was happening before their eyes. The end of their known Universe had taken place and it was no comfort that this had been part of their cultural expectations.

The Space Ark had successfully crossed vast distances of interstellar space and this stood as a great testament to the scientists and engineers who had designed and created the craft. The navigation system had been set to arrive at a new home planet identified as a good bet for being capable of maintaining human life. Although the landing had been rough there were no serious casualties and the automated systems had deployed successfully to release the human cargo and also expel various technological support systems and devices. Audio broadcasts explained how to use equipment for life support while other mechanisms outlined a brief history of the old Earth. The messages outlined how the sun had emitted deadly radiation and it had become necessary to abandon the planet in a Space Ark spacecraft to seek a new habitable world. Not all of the people would listen to or accept such wild stories, though some did. The latter were the potential leaders of the survivors.

Issues around who might become leaders were for the future. The business of surviving in the new landscape and assessing what was happening were the first priorities.

Terra Nova turned out to be an excellent choice. Life had started there independently and taken its own evolutionary pathway. However, there were no higher animals. Pale green grass-like matter coated the ground and sustained itself by photosynthesis. The latter process had emitted breathable oxygen into the air as a by-product and light winds gently swirled the air. There were supplies of liquid freshwater in pools on the surface and in layers below the topsoil. These were replenished by regular build ups of grey clouds which precipitated life giving aqueous precipitation in the form of heavy raindrops at fairly regular intervals. Incoming radiation levels from space were below lethal values though they were a little higher than on the old Earth. A protective ozone layer high up in the atmosphere generated a bluish tinge in the daytime sky. Temperatures generally were not extreme and varied in the range of twenty five to thirty five degrees Celsius in the daytime at the location of the landing site. At night the temperature dropped to about four degrees so the people would need to find ways of keeping warm to maintain their comfort and health. The planet was somewhat hotter at its equator and had cool polar caps containing both water ice and frozen carbon dioxide. The daily rhythm moved in twenty five hour cycles though true darkness never fell at night. There were occasional ground quakes and volcanic activity but these were very rare and mild.

The main feature giving the landscape its own unique fingerprint was the frequent pockmarking caused by ancient asteroid and meteorite collisions. Some craters were twenty to thirty miles across but there were also numerous small pits just a few feet in diameter. Most of the landscape was flat but for some unknown geological reason in the east the ground became hilly and this expanded into a localised mountain range extremely limited in its range. There were no vast brine oceans or running watercourses and the landscape was relatively barren.

The ability of the designers of the Space Ark to think ahead provided the newly landed human population with various technological 'tool-kits' which would, if needed, generate and purify water. There were also various 'cloning kits' which could be activated to generate terrestrial edible plants and replicate meat proteins. It was up to the people now freed from the great ship to learn, understand and use everything they had been given. Their lives and the future of mankind depended on it.

Red and blue wristbands mingled as differences were set aside. Only time would tell if past social divisions would ultimately resurface once again within human society. For now, all the humans were too shocked at the events into which they had been thrown to consider inter-religious alienation though it is true to say a few individuals suspected the opposite community of contriving what had happened. In the short term at least, there would be mutual co-operation.

The social scenario between Muons and Pions reflected an aspiration that had been expressed many years before in the distant past where an attempt was made to unite mankind against a common enemy. In 1987, President Ronald Reagan addressed the United Nations in a speech. He spoke of world unity that would happen if aliens invaded the Earth. He said: *"Perhaps we need some outside universal threat to make us recognize this common bond. I occasionally think how quickly our differences worldwide would vanish if we were facing an alien threat from outside this world."* The Muons and Pions had encountered their own 'universal threat'.

CHAPTER 12

The Return: an Old Earth

Despite her problems escaping from the landed Space Ark, Sylvie had eventually managed to force her way into the time portal device. John had set the device up in such a way as to distinguish between the individuals that passed across its interface into the great void of a wormhole where the existence of time and space were tweaked. Sylvie had joined her husband at the co-ordinates he had pre-set for her in terms of both location and time. Sylvie and John were re-united in the past. They decided to take what might be last looks at their son and granddaughter.

John and Sylvie had made their rendezvous at Kevin's house. They agreed to leave Kevin sleeping and managed to enter the house without disturbing him. While he slept, Sylvie and John spent a short time observing their son. They also took a look at their grandchild Amy sleeping peacefully in her bed in a room along the landing. Their visit was brief. They did not want to disturb Kevin or Amy. Waking them would complicate things too much. It was better not to reveal their presence. The future of Kevin and Amy was one which did not require or involve their participation. They had plans for their own lives and had decided that so much 'water had flowed under the bridge' that Kevin and Amy should be left alone without further interference.

The handle on the door turned. The movement was so slow, it was almost imperceptible. Amy lay in her bed, sleep washing over her tired eyes. She heard a slight noise as the door handle rotated. It seemed that her bedroom door had opened just sufficiently to result in a minor gap appearing between the door and frame on the wall. Her sleep had been disturbed. She could not think who would want to enter her room as it was very early in the morning and barely light. Thin rays of sunlight penetrated the curtains covering the glass windows. Amy was still very sleepy. Even as a child she would not have believed that that her granddad and grandmother had arrived from the future and were taking a peek. For sure, something had woken Amy from her slumbers. Assuming she had imagined what she thought she had seen, she went back to sleep.

Amy was just eight years old. She had few memories of her earlier life as a younger child. Any effort to recall former events would result in hazy scenes and confused thoughts. Her young imagination would not have been able to grasp the idea of having been born in the future and brought into the past to live with her dad. However, Amy was in very good health and had few misgivings about her lack of early memories. She lived in the present and did her best to have fun and enjoy life. Amy was the apple of her dad Kevin's eye. Kevin spoiled his daughter though he rigorously taught her respect for others and politeness to empower her in later life. Any taunts from school friends about her lack of a mother at home were countered by her comments on the quality of parenting being more important than the number of parents indoors. For his part, Kevin did not like talking to his daughter about her mother and Amy considered it to be an issue to be brought up at some time in the future. It was not something that weighed heavily on her mind.

The bedroom door quietly closed but the sound was loud enough and real enough for Amy's ears to detect. Amy pulled the warm duvet fully over her head to hide from whatever was scaring her. She exposed her right eye. Nothing unusual was visible. Who was outside her room? Amy bravely decided to get out of bed and take a look. She did not want to disturb her dad. She could hear him snoring in his room at the end of the landing. Amy gingerly tiptoed to the bedroom door. She took a deep breath and gripped the door handle. In one swift continuous move she pulled the door open. She had prepared her mind to find a frightening bogeyman outside her door. No-one was there.

Kevin had faint memories of a time when he felt he had existed in the future. The Earth in those days was a very strange and changed place. He was unsure if these were real or false memories. They had a dreamlike quality to them. Kevin had visions of meeting the dad he had not known in his childhood and could even put a name to him. He was called John. Kevin still felt affection for his wife Jane but she had left him and he had to raise their daughter Amy on his own. He harboured the strange feeling that he would one day meet up with Jane again and they would get back together.

Kevin remembered his childhood days as good times and being brought up by his loving mum Sylvie. Something had happened to her and he felt he had been accused of harming her. The idea was preposterous. He felt that his mum had also existed in the strange future time on the Earth. Many of these thoughts were confused but these weird memories were embedded into his brain whether they were real or not.

Jane's journey through the time portal had taken a different route to that of Sylvie. She emerged successfully into the old Earth at a date after John and Sylvie had paid a visit to Kevin's house when Amy was still a child. Although seemingly an anomaly, the time-course of events were intertwined versions of each other which had taken various twists and turns depositing Jane at a different temporal co-ordinate at a point when Amy had gone past her early childhood years and had matured.

New memories returned to and filled Jane's mind while some of the past memories that had already returned meandered through her brain. She felt they were based on reality rather than fantasy. Each time a memory repeated itself it revealed more details or clarity. Jane recalled that she had courted and married Kevin. She had been deeply in love with her husband.

Jane's mind swept back and forth. There was one outstanding event in her head which she tried to block out. Jane remembered the time that the birth of her child was imminent. The early signs of labour had started and she had been with Kevin in the family car with the intention of driving to the hospital where she would give birth. A dreamlike scenario followed. She had passed through a triangular device. Lights flashed red, green and blue as she passed through an aperture. She had emerged on the other side into a very strange place. Was this a real place or a dreamed up view? Something had floated in front of her as a silhouette against the background of a dark red sun which stood out against a virtually starless and cloudless black sky.

What was that object that had been hovering in front of the strange sun? Had it spoken to her? Had she heard a voice in her head? The object floating nearby had the form of an owl. It was an old, kind and wise one. She had followed it. Jane now realised that this did not make any sense. In her mind's eye she stared hard at the beautiful owl and it slowly metamorphosed its structure into something different. She now knew that there had never been an owl. She realised that the figure belonged to John, Kevin's dad. The owl had been an illusion. Jane had followed what she had seen as the benevolent owl and entered a large spherical building with a dome and prostrated herself on some kind of floating surgical table.

She had given birth to a daughter. Kevin was there. He declared that their child was called Amy. Jane's memories were very fluid at this point and she was not certain of what happened next. She felt that Kevin had taken her daughter away from her and she had become upset. Around this time she had entered some kind of storage tank or vat and her existence within this container was very blurred. Some of the memories seemed rather outlandish. She had strange visions of being stored nude in a vat. The events she had subsequently experienced crystallized in Jane's mind. She had been released from the vat and had found herself in a strange place but she was not alone. Her mother-in-law Sylvie had been there and someone else. Oh yes, it was Kevin's dad. This seemed very odd. Some strange people had suddenly appeared and captured them but they had later escaped.

Jane recalled how she had entered a time portal device. Her thoughts had been concentrated on finding her daughter and husband in the past. This is what she now needed to do. Her memories and thought processes had reached a point of sufficient understanding such that she could cope and get on with her search for Amy and Kevin.

Amy might now be grown up depending on any time anomalies that may have occurred during her passage through the vortex of the wormhole but it did not matter too much to Jane. Even if she had missed out on Amy's childhood, she was confident that Kevin would have nurtured her. It would be better to meet her daughter even if she was at a matured stage of life rather than as a baby. It would be better than not knowing her at all.

Jane hoped she would be able to see a physical resemblance in Amy to herself. This would provide a visible link between them, an undeniable connection with the baby that had been taken away from her. Jane was not pretentious but she knew she herself possessed good looks. She was sure she would be able to recognise herself within her daughter's features. After all, fifty per cent of Amy's genetic make up came from her.

Jane had arrived safely on the old Earth. Her mental faculties were intact. She quickly set about the task of finding Kevin and her long lost daughter.

CHAPTER 13

The Future in the Present

John exerted mind control over Kevin. The man from the future dominated his son's mental processes utilising the implant technology present in Kevin's neck. After Kevin had delivered Amy on her birth in the futuristic Earth, John instructed Kevin to return to the old Earth through the time portal to resume his everyday life. He informed Kevin that when Amy reached the biological age of eight years old she would be passed back in time into his care where she would remain until she attained reproductive maturity at which point she would be needed for the Great Plan.

Jane recalled John telling her about the Great Plan and the proposed involvement of his granddaughter in it. He hoped that drastic genetic engineering manipulations he carried out on the young developing Amy might result in her becoming sufficiently genetically altered to withstand the rigors of the harsh environment in the future Earth. Kevin somehow had found sufficient mental capacity and protective paternal drive to resist the future life pathway for his daughter planned by John. He argued with his father against it. Jane approved of her husband standing up to his father's wishes.

Jane was aware that John had duly undertaken genetic manipulation experiments on Amy and this could now not be changed. A most unusual change of heart had suddenly and unexpectedly taken place. Changing his mind was not a common feature of John's behaviour. It was neither typical of John nor of others that had lived on the future Earth. A vestige of human emotion lay buried deep down in John's psyche. Love was not extinct in the humans living in the future but it had been suppressed. These thoughts were supplemented by a feeling of pride in his son for his willpower in resisting his implant's efforts to influence and reduce his capacity to think for himself. Kevin had argued a good case in his attempt to change John's plans for Amy. Jane had not yet forgiven her father-in-law for tinkering with her daughter's genes but at least she was alive and well with her dad. Jane would finally get her chance to play a role in her daughter's life despite missing out on her childhood.

The sun shone bright yellow in a cloudless blue sky. A soft breeze ruffled Jane's long blonde hair. Jane stood within a woodland setting amid ancient oaks and younger beech and hornbeam trees. Clusters of *Dryopteris* ferns clumped together in the shade bearing their sori spore cases on the underside of their leaflike fronds. The spores would soon dehisce and be released and dispersed by air currents. Some would fall onto fertile soil and germinate while those falling onto a dry or hostile substratum would not survive. This was the old Earth.

The woodland environment triggered memories in Jane's mind of happy times in the past when she had frolicked with Kevin in the local woodland at the time they were single. This was another place at another time yet Jane felt comfortable within her current surroundings. She followed what looked like a track made by small animals, perhaps rabbits, through a diverse range of shrubs and bushes. Before long the track opened out onto a pathway which was clearly caused by the trampling of plants by the footwear of human walkers and ramblers. The more she walked the more Jane's mind cleared. She would soon meet her daughter for the first time and tell her how much she had missed her and how beautiful she had grown.

Jane continued along the trampled path and then turned off the track to traverse a field of cut maize, leaving the trees and shrubs of the woodland behind her. Jane headed for some small buildings in the distance which appeared to be a farm complex with outbuildings, barn and a thatched farmhouse. As Jane continued on her way it became clear that the farm was actively being worked. Fields of potatoes and cabbages were in view.

The farm yielded its secrets to Jane as she came into close proximity. One of the buildings was a stable which appeared to be home to several horses who peered out of their pens to see who was approaching. A nearby converted barn contained a number of show jumping fences set at very low heights. It seemed likely that this area was used as a riding school to teach young people how to ride, control a horse and make safe jumps.

Jane trekked onwards. No people were in view. A sign caught her eye which hung precariously on a pole above the entrance into a rundown wooden building. The sign proclaimed 'Farm Shop' and Jane could make out various products inside. As well as jams, honey and wines there were sacks of potatoes and 'free range' eggs. Prices were listed on a poster attached to a wall and there appeared to be an 'honesty box' sitting on a very old oak table. Presumably the shop was not always staffed and visitors were invited to take what they wished and leave their payment in a wooden money box which sat astride the rickety table.

Just beyond the Farm Shop Jane noticed a small cross with an inscription. There appeared to be a small grave. An engraved metallic plaque was anchored below the crosspiece. It read "Bullet, our faithful dog and friend. R.I.P." It seemed a rather sad sight to Jane but it was a nice gesture of the dog's owners to remember a family pet. Having stopped to take a moment out of her time to bless Bullet with a quick prayer, she continued walking, following her quest to meet her lovely daughter. She hoped her arrival would not turn out to be an overwhelming emotional experience or great shock to Amy and that she would in time be able to return emotions to her mother and ultimately love her. Jane also was in awe of meeting Kevin again. She had loved him so much. She now knew that many of her husband's actions had been instigated by the implant in his body which influenced him according to his dad John's wishes.

Jane continued on her way to a wooden gate held in place by rusting hinges which separated the property from the narrow country lane outside. On the gate was pinned a corroded metallic plate saying 'Mitchell's Farm'. The outside lane was not tarmac but rather a muddy track along the centre of which sprouted stunted grasses and weeds. This rural lane would not take regular or heavy traffic. It would only see an occasional mail van, tractor or hay cart traversing its winding route.

Jane slid past the farm gate and turned right. She walked as fast as she could. Her nerves were now beginning to take a toll. Her heart was racing and beads of sweat dripped down her cheeks from her brow. Was she really about to see her beautiful daughter? How would she react? Would Amy be shocked or shed tears of joy? How would Kevin react to seeing her after such a long time? Her own emotions were beginning to go into meltdown. Jane could feel the tension building but she struggled to keep her self-control. Within five minutes the lane took a sharp bend to the left. On the outside of the bend was a small cottage with whitewashed walls and a thatched roof. Jane knew she had arrived. This place might become her new home. Jane stood still and surveyed the scene. An expensive looking car was parked next to the property. It seemed Kevin had not endured any financial hardship despite his own complex life history. Jane took a few deep breaths and proceeded to the front door.

Jane grasped the horseshoe-shaped door knocker and gave two sharp thumps. There was no immediate effect and Jane felt like she had been waiting at the door for an age. She was considering knocking again when she heard a rustling sound from within the house. The door creaked and groaned as it was slowly pulled wide open from within. Standing before Jane was Kevin. Jane felt frozen. She could not move or talk. Kevin looked older, slightly more rotund and had wisps of grey in his hair. However, there was no doubting it… it was him. Kevin for his part looked equally in awe at Jane. The married couple made eye to eye contact but neither of them could speak. They simply stood and observed each other face to face. A minute of silent staring ensued which felt like an eternity to both of them. Jane felt her lips quivering. She was trying to speak but no words would issue forth from her dry mouth. As for Kevin, he turned as white as the proverbial sheet. His pupils were dilated.

Jane mouthed some words but nothing audible was transmitted. Eventually a tear escaped from Jane's left eye and very slowly took a winding course down her cheek. She heard herself sounding a murmur which limited itself to "K… K…K…"

"Jane!" said Kevin. "Is it really you? Jane! My Jane! My wife! Oh!" With that, Kevin took a step forward and put his arms around his wife. Jane melted into his warm body and burst into tears.

"Kev! Oh Kevin. I do not have the words to tell you what is going on in my mind."

Kevin took Jane inside the house and sat her down. Their conversation ranged over many events, some old pleasant memories and other more disturbing things that had happened, mainly in the future Earth. The overall picture of their lives was not quite as confused as it might have been. The exposure of both Kevin and Jane to contact and discourse with his dad had filled in many of their life experience memories which might otherwise have been missing or shrouded in mystery. Kevin who still retained his implant explained how his dad had manipulated his life and his actions though Jane did possess some prior knowledge of this. Jane had also received a degree of telepathic programming from Kevin's dad even though she had her implant removed by surgery during a neck vertebra operation. They both had a reasonable grasp of what had happened to them in the future Earth.

Kevin explained how he had become an automaton and in a robotic way had been forced to abduct his own wife and deliver their daughter in a future time zone. He had been induced to place an implant device in Amy's neck to ensure John could control her and bring her back to the future Earth after his genetic tinkering was complete. Although Amy had been sent back to the old Earth to live with Kevin he dreaded that one day his father would remove her and use her or her children as a guinea pig(s) for human survival in the future world. Kevin had been a great dad and Amy had grown and matured under his care. Unexpectedly, Kevin eventually learned that his appeals to his dad John to allow Amy to continue her life on the old Earth eventually succeeded.

For her part, Jane discussed her storage in a technological vat which had maintained her body in good health for many generations and how the building which had been the main feature of the future Earth took on its other role as a spacecraft. Eventually she was 'released from stasis' and learned that the 'future is now'. Jane explained that she had been released into the company not only of John but also Sylvie, Kevin's mum. Jane outlined to Kevin their capture by hostile folk calling themselves Muons and Pions who had been socially thrown together when the great spacecraft set down on a new home-world, expelling all the humans.

Jane explained that she, Sylvie and John had vacated the craft via a time portal device. She assumed that Sylvie and John were together somewhere, perhaps in a different time zone or spatial location, or both. She had been relocated to different co-ordinates in order to try and restart a life with Kevin and meet Amy. Here she was.

At this point the tension in Jane's voice became evident. Kevin had not said too much about Amy. Where was she? When could she meet her? Had John's genetic engineering affected her? Jane was past caring, she just wanted to meet her daughter and hug her.

To Jane's surprise, Kevin stood up and said that she could meet Amy immediately. She was somewhat shy and had been keeping out of sight in the adjacent living room listening intently to the conversation flowing back and forth between her parents.

"Amy! Come in and meet your mother. She has waited a long time for this moment."

Jane stood up in anticipation. She wondered if Amy had inherited any of her own good looks.

Amy floated into the room. Jane heard a distinct telepathic 'voice' resonating inside her head.

"So nice to meet you mother" said Amy, utilising her powers of non-verbal telepathic communication.

Jane fixed her gaze on her long lost daughter. Amy was four feet tall. Her head was bulbous and enlarged. It boasted a completely hairless pate. Her eyes were expanded, slanted and jet black but no sign of eyelids or eyebrows were evident. Amy's chin was thin and pointed and her mouth was only indicated by a narrow slit without lips. Little was present in the way of a nose though two orifices represented vestigial nostrils. No external ear structures were visible but there were vestigial external openings on each side of the head. Amy's bodily torso was very frail looking and lacked musculature. There was no sign of breast development. Her arms were longer than might have been expected compared to her spindly legs. Amy's fingers were long and slender and she moved as if in slow motion.

John had done a great job manipulating her genes and adapting his granddaughter to the low gravity and reduced light intensity of the future Earth. Her thick grey-blue skin would have protected her from the red sun's harmful emissions on the future Earth…had she lived there.

After a short pause Jane addressed her daughter.

"You are beautiful" she said.

ACKNOWLEDGEMENTS

I would like to thank my friends Evelyn Mukahiwa and Wei Wei Cheng (Vivian) for their support, inspiration and enthusiastic encouragement. Further acknowledgements go out to other friends past and present including Keith Major, Bahram Moradbakhti, Zvonko Kazlevski (Zak) and Joleen Allard. It is impractical to name everybody here so please forgive me if your name is excluded.